T
Zombie C.....

ZC ONE

Chris Harris

Dear Reader

I do hope you enjoy reading this book, but I feel I should warn you that, unlike my series UK DARK, which contains few profanities and limited descriptive violence, this book is different.

For the sake of realism there are frequent uses of the "F word" and the violence and gore is obviously more graphic. If this upsets you, then I am sorry, but in my defence, I think you would be hard pressed to find anyone under imminent threat of being eaten by a zombie who wouldn't swear profusely!

Thank you for your understanding.

Chapter one

WOLFE MEDICAL RESEARCH LABORATORY,
BIRMINGHAM, ENGLAND

"It works, it bloody works! Yes! We've done it!" Professor Andy Lawrence shouted, his eyes fixed on the screen in front of him.

He was Chief Scientist at Wolfe Medical, a small, privately funded research laboratory where the past eight years had been spent striving to develop a genetically modified "virus killer". Thousands of failed attempts had been made to develop a carefully altered rhinovirus (common cold virus) that would attach itself to a living virus in a cell and turn it into a harmless replica of itself. This process would continue until all virus cells were destroyed.

It would then lie dormant in the body until another strain of the rhinovirus was detected, when it would spring into action, modifying itself to match the new variant and starting all over again.

On the screen, small spiky blobs could be seen meeting and linking with other spiky blobs and then moving off to begin the process again.

"This," said Andy, "is the twentieth different serotype this beauty has attacked and rendered harmless."

His "second in command", Professor Ian Devey, sat beside him and stared at the screen, lost for words. More staff gathered round as word spread quickly around the laboratory.

This was the Holy Grail of viral research, Nobel Prize winning medicine, and they were all part of it. Careers had been made by moments like this. Once the silent wonder of what they were witnessing had passed, and realisation of their achievement had sunk in, the celebrations began.

The serious lab technicians and research assistants abandoned their usual reserve and began to cheer and clap. Shouting to make himself heard over the noise, Ian shook Andy's hand, "You must tell Mr Wolfe, he needs to know about this."

Andy shook his head, "I can't yet, Ian. I need to run more tests. Come on man, you know good research can't be rushed. I'll tell him as soon as we're sure it really works. We both know what he's like. He only wants positive results, not maybes. Another couple of months or so and then we'll tell him."

Disappointed, Ian nodded, "Of course, let's not get his hopes up. Shall we call it a day? It's two o'clock on a Friday afternoon. We won't get this lot back to work, so let's all finish early and I'll buy the first round in the pub."

"If you promise to buy the second one as well, I'll get this place cleared in ten minutes," Andy replied grinning.

Later on in the pub, Rose, one of the research assistants, typed a short message into her mobile phone, pressed send and put the phone back into her pocket. No one took any notice. Why would they? Texting was such a normal everyday activity.

Looking back, it was this moment that began the process by which human beings would cease to be the dominant species on the planet, and would become the hunted.

Chapter two

Late that evening, Andy and Ian left the pub and made their way unsteadily back to the penthouse city centre apartment they shared.

Over the past eight years the research had taken over their lives. Both men had been married, and within six months of each other, both their wives had filed for divorce, citing abandonment as the main reason. To combat the unhappiness they'd felt, the two men had responded in the only way they knew how; by throwing themselves into their research even more.

Once both divorces were finalised, they had found themselves house hunting at the same time. They'd reached the following conclusion: as they worked together for twelve hours a day, often found themselves eating together after work rather than eating alone, and were both far more interested in their research than in the opposite sex, they might as well live together as confirmed bachelors.

To begin with, they'd rented a small two bedroomed apartment, but once Mr Wolfe had realised how many more hours they were spending at the laboratory and the advances they were making in their research, he'd seized the opportunity of renting the nearest available penthouse apartment on their behalf as a "thank you" for their efforts.

Andy grabbed at a lamp post for some support, swayed and looked up at the office block that housed their research laboratory.

"We forgot to turn the lights out," he noted, slurring slightly.

Ian, just as unsteady on his feet, replied, "I'm not doing it now. I'll do it in the morning."

They continued to make their way home.

Had they been more sober, they might have noticed the car parked outside the office block. The dark rear windows made it impossible to see Mr Wolfe, the laboratory's sole benefactor, watching them from within. A smile flickered across his face as the sight of the two friends, helping each other home after one too many drinks, stirred up distant memories from a time long past.

Mr Wolfe was a nondescript man in his late fifties. He possessed the ability to make the best Saville Row suit look like a charity shop cast-off. This camouflage, perfected over the years, had led many a competitor to underestimate his abilities. The empire he had built up spanned continents and countless industries, from hotels to fishing, and from oil exploration to diamond mines. He seemed to have the golden touch, and over the past three decades, had put together a truly impressive portfolio.

Outwardly everything looked perfect. He had the empire, the yachts, the houses and cars that everyone expected him to have. He was seen at all the right events and regularly featured in high-profile magazines. But he was a worried man.

His hand shook slightly as he picked up his mobile phone and re-read the text he had received earlier, during a meeting with his main creditor. The man, who had been demanding to know when Wolfe would be meeting the next instalment on the huge mountain of debt he had amassed, had watched open-mouthed as, without hesitation, Wolfe had stood up and walked out of the room.

The words "Viable virus ready" were illuminated on the screen.

He had started to fund the laboratory when everything seemed to be going well for him. A bit of philanthropy had appealed to him.

Funding a medical research laboratory would make him look good, give him the right kind of profile, and encourage more people to invest in his business deals.

At first he'd shown no interest in the results; the laboratory was just a way of helping to raise more money.

But then he'd realised the potential of what they were working on. The wealth and fame that such a medical breakthrough could bring to the person who delivered it to the world, would be incalculable.

Then came the global downturn that he'd confidently assumed would never touch him. Instead, it had dealt him blow after blow. Oil wells ran dry, factories closed due to poor order books and hotels sat empty, as governments discouraged their citizens from travelling to certain countries due to terrorist threats. His business empire, which had always seemed so solid and unshakeable, proved to have an Achilles heel. As his debt increased, so did his inability to pay it off.

He should perhaps have closed the Wolfe Medical Research Laboratory, as a vanity he could ill afford. But deep down he felt it might prove to be the saving of him and it gave him a credible air of respectability in the current financial market, which he sorely needed.

And let's face it, another couple of million a year of debt was neither here nor there, given the amount of trouble he was already in.

As the retreating pair turned the corner and disappeared from view, he stepped from the rear of the car and walked to a service door around the side of the building. As owner of the office block he had already procured the access keys and security codes for the entire place. While he had been waiting for Ian and Andy to leave the pub and go home, he had used his tablet computer to disable the CCTV system for the building.

There must be no record of him ever having been there.

He had visited the laboratory many times and knew his way around. He made straight for the storage safe, where the viruses were stored in specialised metal containers that kept them frozen at a specific temperature. Quickly identifying the right one, he donned thick gloves, opened it up and removed two vials containing the genetically modified virus.

He took out a second, smaller container from the bag he had been carrying, and placed the vials carefully inside.

After locating Lawrence's computer, he overrode his security code with his own, which had already been embedded into the software, and finding Lawrence's research notes, copied them over to a memory stick which he had inserted into the USB drive.

On his way out of the laboratory, he made his one mistake. Instinctively, he switched off the lights as he closed the door and locked it. He made his way down the emergency stairs and was soon back in his car. He was out of breath from the exertion, but felt more alive than he had in months. He was reminded of the few shady deals he had been involved in when he had started his empire, and the rush that you got when you knew you had succeeded.

He instructed his chauffeur to take him to an airfield just outside London, where he had arranged for his private jet to be fuelled and waiting for him.

Chapter three

As the car pulled up alongside, the sleek jet's engines began to whine as the pilot prepared for take-off. Wolfe boarded the plane, and having made sure that the bag was secured, poured himself a large drink from the bar. He settled himself back into one of the luxurious seats and waited for the familiar sensation of being pressed back into it, as the plane accelerated down the runway.

As soon as the wheels had left the ground, he closed his eyes and smiled to himself. The first part of his plan was complete; now for part two. In an ideal world he would, of course, have waited for Lawrence to complete the testing and confirm that his "wonder cure" for the common cold really worked, before releasing the news to the world. The problem was, he didn't have the time. He needed results now. He needed the banks and financiers to see what he had created.

They would, Wolfe reasoned, instantly recognise the value of what he had, and the money would start to pour in again as they all clamoured for a piece of it. For a share in his success. He simply couldn't afford to wait for months, or even years, of rigorous testing before the product could be deemed fit for human trials. "Maybes" didn't impress the banks anymore. Guaranteed successes did.

He had been planning this for a long time. A few years before, he'd bought an old Soviet era military base on the shores of the Black Sea in the Ukraine.

The plan had been to redevelop it as a luxury holiday resort for the "up and coming" middle classes of the old Soviet bloc countries, not the ones who seemed to fill most of the fashionable European resorts these days, but the ones who aspired to do so, and would therefore willingly accept the slightly cheaper option offered at his resort. The resort had been another spectacular failure.

Having spent tens of millions buying the place and bribing government officials to speed up the development process, the civil war had started in the Ukraine, rendering his two thousand acres of prime Black Sea frontage property virtually worthless. Rose had proved a useful informant inside the laboratory and well worth the substantial sum of money he had paid her. When she had confirmed that Lawrence was close to success, he had lost no time in fitting out an empty building on the old base as a laboratory, and engaging a number of scientists who cared more about money than ethics, to be on standby to travel there as soon as he notified them.

Their instructions had been to take the virus sample from him, and using the research data uploaded from Lawrence's computer, to rush it through the final stages of testing, if necessary, fabricating some evidence to prove that it worked.

Dawn was breaking as the jet touched smoothly down on the runway at the abandoned base.

One of the scientists who had already arrived at the base entered the plane and took the bag and memory stick from Mr Wolfe. Leaving the plane, he walked the short distance across the runway to the laboratory. By the time the jet had taken off, he'd already transferred the vials into large cold-storage canisters and uploaded the research notes on to his computer.

Mr Wolfe slept soundly all the way back to England. He would need all his energy to get through the next week or so until he could announce his medical breakthrough to the world. Inside millions of deep frozen cells within the vials, the virus waited patiently, a genetically engineered weapon, designed to modify itself and kill the many strains of rhinovirus that caused seventy five percent of colds globally.

It was going to save employers billions of pounds annually by reducing sick days and increasing productivity.

It was the most efficient killing machine on a cellular level ever invented by man.

So efficient that within two weeks, humanity would be an endangered species.

Chapter four

Lawrence and Devey were back in the laboratory early the next morning, not quite as early as usual, admittedly, as they were both feeling rather delicate after the previous day's celebrations.

They had both forgotten about the lights being left on the night before and immediately occupied themselves with their work. They concentrated on testing and re-testing the results under various controlled conditions, methodically working their way through the robust and seemingly endless process of testing the modified virus killer.

By Tuesday morning all the scientists had presented themselves at the laboratory in the Ukraine. The early arrivals quickly brought the rest up to speed on what they had discovered so far. Everyone was impressed and acknowledged that a remarkable breakthrough had been made. In direct contravention of all the rules and guidelines, testing commenced straightaway on primates.

Twenty rhesus macaque monkeys were already housed in cages in a room next to the laboratory.

One monkey was infected with a strain of rhinovirus, then placed in a cage in isolation in another room.

A second monkey was injected with the modified virus and placed in the same cage as the first, along with a third, untreated monkey. The following day the monkey that had received the rhinovirus was showing cold-like symptoms. The day after the test, the untreated monkey was also showing symptoms. The monkey that had received the modified virus was displaying no symptoms at all.

The blood samples taken clearly showed that in the monkey with the modified virus, the rhinovirus had not developed at all. The scientists were ecstatic.

So far, the research they were being paid a great deal of money to undertake had been easy.

It worked. All that remained was for them to take the credit for someone else's work. Carried away with excitement and greed, the lead scientist, Vladimir Petrov, contacted Mr Wolfe. For one million pounds, he would volunteer to be the first human test subject. Without hesitation, Mr Wolfe agreed. How could he not? Within five days of the virus being perfected, it was going to be tested on a willing human subject.

Twenty minutes after Petrov had received confirmation that the money was in his bank account, a colleague injected him with the modified virus and they all left the laboratory for one of their regular cigarette breaks.

The base was surrounded by coastal marshland where several small rivers emptied themselves into the vastness of the Black Sea. The marsh was a natural habitat for several species of rare local wildlife, and subsequently also an ideal breeding ground for mosquitos.

Mr Wolfe had been aware of this, and not wanting swarms of blood-sucking insects ruining his guests' holidays, had planned to drain the land and turn it into the resort golf course.

He had paid enough bribes to the local government bureaucrats to combat any environmental concerns about the destruction of such an important natural habitat.

Vladimir sat in the sun and enjoyed his cigarette, oblivious to the virus coursing through his veins, and contemplated his future as a millionaire.

As the sun began to set, he never felt the bite on his neck as a mosquito from the marshes landed gently and fed on his blood.

There's no way of telling what virus the mosquito was carrying.

It's highly likely that during the testing period, Lawrence would have identified the fault with his creation, put a few more months of intensive work in and redesigned his virus-killer to rectify the problem.

Instead, the unknown virus entered the scientist's bloodstream and encountered the genetically engineered rhinovirus. The rhinovirus attached itself to the invading virus, but instead of neutralising it, it altered itself. The new mutated virus was never given a name.

In the few weeks it took for it to wreak devastation on the human race, the few survivors had more important things to worry about.

After another hour's work, the scientists finished up and went to the hotel in the nearby village where they would be staying until the contract was completed. They ate their evening meal together, and after a few drinks in the bar, they all retired for the evening. Vladimir was too excited to sleep. He lay on his bed, his mind racing. He was a millionaire, with more money than he'd ever dreamed of. By nature a selfish man, any thoughts about the others and his obligation to complete the work went out of the window.

Why was he wasting his time in this backwater of a town, when he could be living the life he deserved with a pretty girl on his arm? His mind made up, he reached for his tablet computer and checked the flights from the local airport.

There was a flight to Moscow first thing in the morning and from Moscow, within hours, he would be in one of the major transport hubs of Europe.

By the following day he could be anywhere in the world. Twenty minutes later, the flight to Moscow was booked. In Moscow he would have a two hour wait for his flight to Heathrow.

He hadn't thought any further than that, but figured it would be simple enough to book a hotel for a day or two and plan the rest of his life. He was looking forward to taking things easy from now on.

Quickly, he packed his belongings, threw his bag on to the backseat of his car and drove off to catch his flight. As he drove along he suddenly sneezed.

He grinned to himself, thinking, *"Well at least I won't be coming down with a cold. That'd really put a dampener on things! Must be the dust."*

Inside him the virus was behaving very strangely. It wasn't spreading rapidly around his body. Each time it reproduced, it mutated slightly, but it was only reproducing enough to enable it to survive, not to affect its host too much. Like some predatory creature, it was biding its time.

Chapter five

It was only after breakfast the next morning that Vladimir's colleagues discovered he was gone. Thinking that he'd overslept, they knocked on his door, entered his room and found it empty. Back in the hotel reception the night porter overheard them talking about him, and confirmed that he had seen him drive off in his car hours ago.

Their first thoughts were that some family emergency might have called him away, leaving him no time to inform the rest of them. But it wasn't long before their suspicions were aroused. They were all aware of his new-found wealth and most of them resented the fact that he had thought of volunteering first. Following a hastily convened meeting, the scientists decided to err on the side of caution and wait to see if Vladimir contacted them. They had no wish to antagonise their employer, so they agreed to wait at least twenty four hours before taking any action.

Having come to a decision, they returned to the laboratory to continue fabricating test data.

As the ageing Russian jet heaved itself into the sky, Vladimir smiled to himself. He had only just made the flight in time and had been forced to abandon his car in the passenger drop-off area and sprint to the check-in desk.

He didn't care; he wasn't going to need that clapped-out car again anyway.

He was feeling slightly hot and flushed, but attributed it to the dash through the airport to get to the gate. The flight had left on time so he would have plenty of time to catch his next flight when he arrived in Moscow. Hopefully, he wouldn't have to rush anywhere again for the rest of his life.

An hour into the short two-and-a-half-hour flight, Vladimir was still feeling slightly feverish. He dismissed it, putting it down to a night without sleep and over excitement. He sneezed again.

Tiny droplets of fluid sprayed from his mouth and nose and spread out in an invisible cloud, covering anyone in close proximity with a microscopic layer of virus-filled moisture. The air-conditioning system did the rest, sucking up the droplets and distributing them efficiently around the packed plane. Not everyone was infected, it was purely a matter of chance. But by the time the plane had reached its destination, over eighty five percent of the passengers were playing host to the mutated virus. It continued its silent journey inside their bodies, still developing, but not yet ready to reveal itself to an unsuspecting world. Not just yet.

More than half the passengers on the flight, Vladimir included, were transiting through Moscow Airport and would shortly be scattering to all points of the globe.

They all made straight for their relevant departure lounges to await their next flights. The rest collected their luggage, left the airport and made their way to their final destinations. They were picked up by friends or relatives, collected their own cars or made use of the highly efficient public transport system Moscow was so famous for. More than eighty five percent of them had unknowingly become carriers for the deadly virus, spreading it with every breath, cough or touch.

Vladimir and the seventy other passengers who were waiting for their next flights were heading for twenty different airports in thirteen different countries. Some of them, like Vladimir, would be continuing their journey on a third flight.

By now the virus was spreading from Vladimir and his fellow carriers to many of the other passengers waiting for flights in the departure lounge. If anyone had realised at the time, all the passengers could have been isolated and the virus might have been stopped in its tracks. The threat of infection from the people who had left the airport might also have been contained, or at least controlled.

But once all the passengers had dispersed and continued on their respective journeys, the damage was done: the virus would now multiply exponentially, which is the reason why experts on infectious diseases break into a cold sweat at the thought of international air travel.

Prediction models have been produced by those same experts, showing how one single infected subject could, given the right conditions, infect the majority of the world's population in a very short space of time. The problem was, it was not just one subject now. With almost single-minded efficiency, the virus had infected almost everyone who had come into contact with it.

A few hours later, Vladimir boarded a British Airways flight to London. Having been the first person infected, he was showing more signs that the others and was starting to feel lousy. Over the course of the four-hour flight, his condition deteriorated, developing rapidly into full blown flu-like symptoms.

His body ached all over and he fluctuated between burning up and experiencing uncontrollable shivering fits. The flight attendants could see that he was ill, but accepted his explanation that it was just a cold that had come on during the morning. They offered him an empty row of seats to sit in, so as not to concern the other passengers, and gave him a few blankets to make him more comfortable.

He'd already booked a room at an airport hotel, hoping to have a nice meal and get an escort to celebrate his new-found status in style. But now all he wanted to do was get to his hotel room and sleep. He was too sick to question what was happening to him or why.

Disembarking at Heathrow, he didn't bother to collect his bag. It only contained clothes and he could easily replace them. Having passed through Customs, he staggered to the bus stop and waited for the shuttle bus that would take him to his hotel.

The virus had been genetically modified for one purpose: to neutralise the one threat to its existence, the rhinovirus. When it had come into contact with the unknown virus from the mosquito bite, a fault in its painstaking programming had emerged. It had encountered a virus with enough similarities in its genetic code to cause a mutation. The two codes had combined to form a new and lethal virus.

The new virus had just one purpose: to replicate and spread. The human immune system is a remarkable thing and under normal circumstances, once a virus has been detected, it will dispatch an army of defender cells, known as lymphocytes, to overpower and disable the invader.

This virus was new; Vladimir's lymphocytes were attacked and changed with devastating effect. They, in their turn, eliminated their only threat: the part of the brain responsible for activating the immune system.

Without an effective immune system to protect it, the virus rampaged through the delicate brain, causing catastrophic damage to the frontal lobe and thereby removing any capacity for experiencing conscious thought or emotions.

Other crucial parts of the brain were also affected. In essence, everything that was responsible for making Vladimir human, was obliterated.

At the same time, a virus is only able to survive in a living, "healthy" host. It made sure of its own survival. The parts of the brain associated with breathing remained intact, so that the cells could continue to receive oxygen. The part of the brain associated with hunger remained untouched, ensuring that the body would seek food in order to survive, and the virus would receive enough energy to reproduce.

The virus had almost run its course and exploded throughout Vladimir's body. Struggling to remain conscious, he almost fell from the bus and staggered into the hotel foyer. Halfway across the foyer he fell to his knees, vomited up the entire contents of his stomach, and collapsed onto the tiled floor.

As Vladimir lay convulsing on the floor in a pool of his own vomit, most people recoiled and stepped back, but a few staff and guests hurried forward to try to help him.

The hotel receptionist phoned for an ambulance and then put out a call for the first-aider on duty to come to reception immediately.

One of the guests, who had been about to leave for the airport with her husband and children, came forward and explained that she was a nurse.

She placed him in the recovery position and set about checking his breathing and vital signs. His breathing was shallow, and his vital signs weak, but he was alive. As the first-aider arrived, the nurse stayed by his side to help until the ambulance turned up.

After handing over to the paramedics, she apologised and explained that she needed to leave or she would miss her flight.

She washed her hands, teeming with virus, in the washbasin in the ladies' toilets and then hurriedly left with her family, another virus carrier created.

By now Vladimir was in a deep state of unconsciousness, his brain all but destroyed by the virus. He was destined never to experience another conscious thought. Now his brain would give him only the most basic abilities and instructions. He was able to breathe, to move and to eat. His sole function would be to identify and move towards a food source. The virus inside him could no longer be spread by coughing and sneezing, and now passed through to the final stage of its transformation.

From now on, in order to be transmitted to another host, it would require contact with a different bodily fluid.

Their blood.

A few moments later, what was left of Vladimir's brain began to function again. Had he possessed the ability to understand language, he would have heard the paramedic saying, "He's coming round, support his head."

All his brain registered was noise.

His empty stomach transmitted an overwhelming sensation of hunger to his brain.

His eyes opened. He could see but he couldn't recognise individuals or objects. His brain was now at its most basic and primal stage of evolution. It was only capable of distinguishing between what was a food source and what was not.

The paramedic leant in closer to examine him. Vladimir emitted a low noise, part groan, part growl, grabbed the unfortunate paramedic by the head and bit deeply into his neck. The urge to feed was overpowering.

Pandemonium broke out.

It was Zombie Apocalypse Day One.

Before too long, thousands of people would be starting to sneeze and the same thought would be running through their minds: *"Oh no, I think I've caught a cold."*

Chapter six

It was a perfect day on Chapel Porth beach. The light breeze felt pleasantly warm in the hot sun and the waves were just the right size for Stanley and Daisy to enjoy bodyboarding without worrying us. I'd spent the last few hours in the surf with them, but now deemed them competent enough to be allowed a bit of freedom, so I returned to Becky, who was sunning herself on a rug on the warm sand.

Ok, I'll admit that the thought of the nice cold beer I had in the cool box had tempted me out of the water. I made sure she was awake by placing my ice cold can of lager on her bare back as I sat down next to her. She screamed and jumped up, ready to fight whoever had dared to wake her up. After I'd defended myself from a few playful slaps, she eventually calmed down and saw the funny side. She grabbed a drink out of the cool box and sat next to me, so that we could chat and keep an eye on the kids.

My name is Tom and I live in Moseley, a suburb of Birmingham, with my wife Becky, and my two kids, Stanley and Daisy. We were spending a few weeks of the children's school holidays visiting the beauty spots of Cornwall in our touring caravan.

The usually fickle and unpredictable British weather had been kind to us, and we'd spent the previous week on Cornwall's beautiful southern coast, pottering around on boats, fishing (unsuccessfully) and visiting the many pretty villages the region is known for, before moving on to the more rugged northern coast, better known for surfing and tin mines.

It was turning out to be a memorable holiday. The kids were having a great time and hadn't yet reached that bored stage where they were likely to start bickering and falling out.

The weather was great and we were all sporting golden tans from being out in the sun all day long. Becky and I were happy because the area was full of great places to eat, which saved all the rigmarole of cooking and cleaning that can sometimes take the edge off a holiday.

What could be better than having a lovely meal, returning to the campsite, and sharing a bottle (or two) of wine, while the children played with their new-found friends? Most evenings were spent reading, watching the sun go down and gazing out at the Wheal Coates tin mine, starkly beautiful in the fading light.

The clamour of children's voices disturbed my peace and I looked up from my Kindle to see Stanley, Daisy and a group of their friends approaching. I remembered that I'd promised them all an ice cream. It looked as if they were coming to collect.

"I'll go and get them," I said, grinning at Becky, and stood up to get the box of ice creams out of the freezer in the caravan.

As I was distributing them, the father of one of the children saw what I was doing and walked over to thank us both. We stood and chatted for a while and then I remembered my manners and offered him a drink and a seat.

He sat down with a glass of wine and introduced himself.

His name was Chris and he was on holiday with his wife and ten year-old son. They had a nice-looking motorhome on the other side of the field, so we spent the first few minutes chatting about the pros and cons of caravans versus motorhomes. A little snigger from Becky stopped us.

"Just listen to you two! Tom, you sound like an old man; you must be boring poor Chris to death, because I'm certainly losing the will to live."

Chris laughed and of course, denied any such thing. The conversation moved on to the kind of topics you tend to discuss with people you're passing the time with on holiday, but know full well you probably won't be seeing again. In typical British fashion the weather was commented on. Then abruptly, Chris changed the subject.

"Did you see the news tonight?" he asked.

"No, we were out. Anything interesting?" I asked.

He shook his head. "Not much. It must have been a slow news day because they reported a cannibal attack at an airport hotel." he replied with a grin. "It sounded to me as if two blokes had a fight and one bit the other. I guess as there wasn't much else going on, they felt they had to make it sound more dramatic."

Chris's wife came over to see where her husband had disappeared to, and naturally we invited her to join us. We spent a further pleasant hour, drinking and chatting, and then it was time to get the children to bed, as we were in danger of losing them in the rapidly descending darkness.

Once the children were settled into their cosy bunk beds, we went back outside and finished our drinks. As Wi-Fi was available on the campsite, I reached for my phone and began checking my emails, deleting any junk messages. Remembering what Chris had said about the cannibal attack, I did a quick search out of idle curiosity.

I navigated my way to the main news websites and tapped in the word "cannibal". This brought up a few reports about an incident at a Heathrow Airport hotel, in which a number of people, including two paramedics who had been attending at an emergency, had been treated for severe bite injuries.

On one of the websites I found a link to some video footage of the event. The footage was shaky and unclear as it had been taken on a mobile phone; in fact, it didn't show anything much apart from screaming people pushing and shoving each other in a bid to escape from something.

Not giving it another thought, I put my phone on charge and we both went to bed.

Chapter seven

Starting with Vladimir Petrov and his colleagues, the infection rate had doubled at every stage of the virus's rapid progress. From the initial one hundred and fifteen infected on Vladimir's first flight from the Ukraine to Moscow, the number was now in the tens of thousands, and growing by the second. It would shortly be affecting millions, as it spread outwards like an unstoppable tide from most major airports.

In spite of being the first place affected, the isolated outbreak at a small Black Sea coastal town went largely unnoticed. It was a small town, separated by the marshes and miles of road from its nearest neighbour.few people visited the resort now that the base had closed down, so the fact that within twelve hours of Vladimir leaving, the entire town had become a mass graveyard and was crawling with zombies would never be known. Had Vladimir not left, the virus might not have spread far.

The government might have discovered the outbreak and although more people would have been infected from bites, a quarantine zone could have been established and under conditions of strict secrecy and a complete media blackout, the problem could have been quietly eradicated, leaving the government scientists with the problem of what to do with a virus which had become a potential weapon.

In the final stages of its evolution the virus had become the perfect killer.

Within minutes of contact the new host also became contagious, and within a few hours, the subject developed severe cold or flu-like symptoms.

Two to six hours after the appearance of these symptoms (depending on their physiological make-up), the host transformed into a zombie.

If you were unfortunate enough to be bitten by a zombie and survived that initial attack, the virus's progression was much more rapid. It took between five and ten minutes for the change to take place, and so the cycle would begin again. Unaware of any of this at the time, Tom had his last night of untroubled sleep.

~

The following morning we had woken to another fine, hot day, so we planned to spend another day on the beach, surfing. After breakfast Becky packed a cool box with drinks and snacks, and I packed the car with body boards, chairs and towels.

The man in the caravan next to us opened his window and shouted to get my attention, "Mate, you gotta see what's happening on the news, it's unbelievable."

The look on his face made me think better of the funny remark I'd been about to respond with. I walked over to his open window and looked at the television, and he turned up the volume.

A visibly shaken news anchor was talking rapidly and urgently, "I repeat, unconfirmed reports are coming in of mobs attacking innocent bystanders at numerous locations around the country. We're trying to contact the police and the Government for a statement, but so far we've had no response. Reports of cannibalism are coming in, again unconfirmed.

But please stay with us as we try to confirm what's happening…" She paused, held her hand to her ear and appeared to be listening to someone through her earpiece. "We can now go live to one of our teams at Central London Hospital." The screen went blank for a moment, then showed a male reporter standing in the car park of a hospital.

"Hello studio, this is Mark Smith and I'm reporting to you live from outside Central London Hospital. I'm not sure what's happening, but reports have reached me of people being attacked at random. I've seen no actual evidence of this yet, as my cameraman and I were returning from filming in the countryside near Oxford when the call came in for us to head here. The one thing I did notice on the way here is how empty the streets are. The London rush hour just hasn't happened. I can't explain it. Also, my car radio doesn't appear to be picking up any stations."

"Oh, come on, this is rubbish. It's not telling us anything!" I complained.

The camera panned out and picked up a few people in the background, stumbling towards the reporter.

The reporter spoke off screen, "I can see some people approaching, I'll go and talk to them and see if they can tell us what's happening."

The camera shook as the cameraman followed the reporter over to a crowd of about ten people. The shot steadied as he stopped and got ready to film the interview. He zoomed in on the nearest person approaching the reporter. It was a man and he was walking awkwardly, as if drunk, but it was the sight of his face that made my blood run cold.

We've all seen zombies depicted in TV shows and films. I was always a huge fan of them, especially the hit US show, "The Walking Dead". So in my mind I had a picture of what a zombie should look like. The reality was far more frightening. His face was grey, pallid and disturbingly blank, dark blood dripped stickily from his mouth and his shirt was torn in several places, revealing horrible looking injuries. Almost absently, I thought to myself, *"Oh! That's a zombie!"*

A millisecond later it sank in properly, "Shit! That's a zombie!"

We watched in horrified fascination as, heedlessly, the reporter walked towards the man, his microphone outstretched in front of him.

The danger dawned on the cameraman much more quickly than on the unfortunate reporter, and we heard him shout a warning, "Mark! Stay away from him!"

Unable to look away, we watched as the reporter thrust the microphone in the man's face. He never got the chance to speak. The "zombie" grabbed the arm holding the microphone and bit into it. The reporter screamed in pain, unable to pull the arm away. The camera seemed to be frozen on the scene of horror as, for a few seconds, the cameraman was clearly unable to process what was happening. Then the view changed, as the cameraman hurriedly put the camera down. In his haste, he must have activated something, because the camera continued to film, at an angle, with the screen now showing a wider view.

With his free arm the reporter was frantically lashing out at his attacker, who showed no reaction and only tightened his hold. The legs, and then the rest of the cameraman appeared in shot, as he hurled himself forward to help his colleague.

There was no sound, (he must have dropped the microphone), but the reporter was soaked in his own blood and his face was contorted in agony, as he screamed silently and tried ever more weakly to free himself.

The cameraman tried desperately to pull the creature away from his friend and we watched helplessly as more "zombies" shuffled unnoticed into view and headed towards the two struggling men.

"Look out!" my neighbour screamed at the screen. We watched, transfixed, as the other zombies literally fell on the two struggling men who, by now, had fallen to the ground. Live on television, we watched as they were literally torn apart and devoured by their attackers.

The view switched abruptly to the studio, as someone had clearly realised that it was too much for people to see. The news anchor sat looking stunned, unable to say anything. The screen went to a commercial break.

My neighbour immediately changed over to BBC One, as that channel offered uninterrupted, commercial-free viewing. The screen showed a message stating that they were experiencing technical difficulties and that normal service would be resumed as soon as possible. He flicked through all the other channels; they all showed the same message.

We looked at each other in shock. What the hell was going on?

I turned and ran into our caravan. The children were still in the playground, waiting for us to tell them when it was time to leave.

"Talking again!" said Becky irritably. "We're supposed to be going out for the day, and all you do is stand around chatting to people. I saw you ..."

I stopped her halfway through her tirade, shouting, "Just shut up! Something fucking weird's going on. I've just watched someone being eaten alive on TV. I need to find out what's happening."

Becky looked at me in shocked silence. We know each other so well she realised immediately that I was deadly serious.

"What?"

"You heard me. I've just seen a news reporter and his cameraman being eaten by other people live on the news."

"Where?"

"Somewhere in London, I think."

I turned the TV and the radio on. The TV was still showing the technical difficulty message, so I tried the radio. None of the pre-set national stations were broadcasting, so I started to scan manually. Without turning round I said, "Go and get the kids NOW, darling."

I managed to find a working station. I didn't know which one it was, but I guess that was irrelevant. The presenter was screaming excitably.

"Please everyone, just listen. I don't know how or what is happening. It's not a joke. I've seen it with my own eyes. Thousands of people have turned into what I can only describe as … zombies … and are attacking everyone.

Please find somewhere safe. I can see them now out of my window. Until the authorities can sort this out, don't, for God's sake, go outside."

He was rambling and speaking ten to the dozen, which made him all the more convincing. It definitely sounded true; he'd have to have been a very good actor to be faking that.

Becky came in, pushing the children in front of her. They were both looking upset and a little bewildered at having their playtime interrupted by an overwrought mother.

As they entered the caravan the presenter shouted, "RUN! For God's sake get away … I'm sorry, I can see someone walking down the street below my studio. I can't get her attention and she's heading straight for them." In the background you could hear the sound of banging on glass. "I can't get her attention. I can't open the windows here. Hold on, I'll try to break the glass. Oh God, she can't hear me!" The banging grew more frantic and then … "Nooooooo!" A few seconds later there was silence, apart from the sound of the presenter retching.

We all stood there, momentarily immobilised by shock. Finally the silence on the radio was broken by the presenter. His voice was quiet this time, hoarse with emotion.

"I'm sorry but I can't begin to describe what I've just witnessed. I can only explain that a crowd of zombies has just slaughtered someone in the street below me. They're still feeding on the poor woman. Jesus Christ!"

He began to cry, "I'm so sorry," he whispered, "I tried to get your attention but you just couldn't hear me." All we could hear then was sobbing, as the man broke down completely.

Becky looked at me, pale as a ghost. "WHAT is going on?"

"You know as much as I do," I replied grimly. "Ten minutes ago that bloke next door called me over because of what he was seeing on TV, and you've just heard what that DJ saw. I haven't got a clue. But the one thing I do know is this is no joke. It can't be. It just can't. But zombies! For fuck's sake! It can't be real."

I saw Stanley smile and look up at me and realised that I'd sworn in front of the children.

"Sorry, Stanley," I added hastily, "just ignore Dad for a bit. I need you both to stay in the van for a little while. I need to have a word with Mommy."

I motioned for Becky to follow me outside. The man from next door was standing on his step having a cigarette. His hand was shaking visibly. He walked over as soon as he saw us.

"The TV's on, but all the channels are just showing an emergency broadcast. It's a message telling everyone to stay at home and avoid contact."

I walked over to his window and looked in at the TV. True enough, a text message was rolling across the screen: "*National Emergency Message. Please stay in your house. Avoid all contact with anyone. Monitor 1050mz on medium wave for information updates.*"

"I've just checked the radio and it's broadcasting the same info," said our neighbour from behind me.

Becky joined us. Looking up, we saw the children watching us anxiously through the caravan window.

"Tom, what's going on, why have all the stations stopped broadcasting?"

"Becky, as I said, you know as much as me. But as crazy as it might sound, we have to believe what we've heard. Somehow or other, there are zombies attacking people. What we need to know is where they are. We have to take this seriously."

My neighbour spoke up, shaking his head. "This is stupid. It can't be happening. It has to be a joke or something. Zombies don't exist!"

"Well you explain what we've just seen and heard then!" I shot back. I would dearly have loved for it to be one big hoax, but somehow I knew it wasn't. I had a gut feeling.

He looked at me. I could see that he wanted to deny what was happening, but his eyes were full of fear. He wanted to believe it was all fake because he didn't want to comprehend the alternative. As we stood there, I thought back to a conversation I'd once had with a group of friends at a dinner party. We'd been talking about the latest films we'd seen and the conversation had turned to the number of zombie films that had been released lately.

I'd joked that it was all to prepare us for a coming apocalypse, so that it wouldn't come as a shock when it finally did happen. I'd laughed and said that we'd be better prepared to defend ourselves, because knowing how to kill a zombie would be an essential bit of information. In short, I'd suggested that all the films were part of a government-sponsored education programme to teach civilians how to survive. Everyone knew, I'd informed them, that you have to destroy the brain to kill a zombie.

I turned to Becky, "Darling, we have to take this thing seriously until we're told otherwise. Look around! This is no place to be if we're attacked. And a caravan won't give us enough protection. We need to get home. I say, we leave the caravan here and go now before panic sets in."

Becky was shocked. "You can't be serious!"

"I am! I say we leave the caravan here and get home as quickly as we can. If it all turns out to be nothing, we can always come back for it in a few days' time."

"What do we tell the kids?"

I thought about it. "The truth, I guess. Because if it is really happening, we'll all need to be prepared."

Chapter eight

Becky and I looked at each other for a moment, then we both ran into the caravan. The children were sitting there quietly. They knew something was wrong.

I took a deep breath then spoke, "Kids, we're going to leave right now and go home. We won't be taking the caravan, so while Mommy and Daddy get things ready, you need to pack your bags with a few clothes and some toys. Becky, pack up as much food and drink as you can, while I throw some of our clothes and some other stuff into a bag."

It didn't take long for me to grab a bag and empty the overhead lockers where we kept our clothes. As I was taking the body boards and towels out of the car, I had the first of many strange conversations with myself. *"If we come across a zombie, what will I kill it with?"*

I hold a shotgun licence and have a number of shotguns at home, so one of those would have been my weapon of choice.

But until we got there and I took them out of my gun-safe, I was going to have to make do with whatever was available. Thinking back to all the zombie films I'd seen, I went and rummaged through the storage locker at the front of the caravan, and took out the broom and a roll of duct tape.

I took the kitchen knives out of the kitchen drawer, and put one in the door pocket of the car. Then I removed the head of the broom, taped a knife to the handle and managed to make a rudimentary spear.

"What on earth are you doing?" said Becky in astonishment, as she emerged from the caravan, carrying a cool box and two bags full of food and bottles of water.

"Making a bloody spear," I snapped, "What do you think I'm doing? Stanley!" I shouted, "Can you find your cricket bat and put it in the back of the car?"

She put the bags down and sighed. "Is this really necessary?" she asked.

"Darling, if this actually turns out to be true, we need to be able to defend ourselves. So unless you can think of another way, I figure it's better to be safe than sorry." With a wry grin on my face I continued, "Twenty minutes ago I was packing body boards. Now I'm making a zombie spear. Let's not talk about what's necessary or not. I think, unless we hear otherwise, normal has just gone out of the window!"

A few minutes later everything had been hastily thrown into the back of our Volvo XC90. Warning the children to be careful of the knife, I put my spear and Stanley's cricket bat on top of the pile.

My neighbour was still outside, pacing backwards and forwards and chain-smoking.

"We're off mate!" I shouted. "Look after yourself, and if it's all a hoax, we'll be back in a few days."

He nodded, a dazed look on his face.

As I started the car, I glanced at the fuel gauge. "Shit!" There was only a quarter of a tank. Nowhere near enough to get home.

"Let's hope the garages are still open," I muttered. "We haven't got enough fuel to get out of Cornwall, let alone home."

As we drove out of the caravan site, it looked as if some of the other families were hurriedly packing their cars. That worried me. "This journey could get interesting. If other people have come to the same conclusion as us about what's going on, we're going to have to be careful. People are capable of doing stupid things when they're panicking."

As I drove as fast as I dared along the narrow lane, Becky tried to find a working station on the radio.

"See if you can find that channel the TV message was on about, 1050 medium wave, wasn't it?"

It didn't take her long to find it. The message had now been replaced by someone making an announcement:

"This is the Emergency Public Broadcast Service for Her Majesty's Government. We have very little information about the current situation, but this is what we know so far. A global virus has broken out.

Victims initially develop cold-like symptoms but then develop severe psychosis. In other words, they become extremely violent and irrational. Reports are coming in of people being attacked and bitten, and the death toll is rising."

The voice paused and then continued. "Please avoid all contact with other members of the public until we can discover more about the situation. Do not travel! Stay where you are. We will continue to provide updates when we can. Monitor this frequency at all times. Until then this message will continue to be repeated."

The message began again, so Becky turned the volume down. We just looked at each other. Daisy, who had been listening to every word, started to cry.

I spotted a petrol station up ahead and slowed to pull in as Becky turned round to comfort her. I breathed a sigh of relief. It appeared to be open. The lights were on and there was a car at one of the pumps. I pulled up alongside one of them, looked round at them and said, "Everyone stay in the car."

The pump had a self-service function, so I inserted my credit card and started to fill the tank. Glancing nervously around, I couldn't see where the other driver was, so I assumed that he or she must be somewhere in the shop or maybe using the toilet.

A few minutes later the tank was full. Replacing the nozzle and retrieving my credit card, I walked around the car to check that everything was ok.

As I could now see the other car from a different angle, I realised that a pair of feet was sticking out from the side of the car. A feeling of unease crept over me. Not wanting to, but knowing that I was going to have to, I crept cautiously over to the car. As I got closer I heard a strange grunting sound. It reminded me of the noise a pig makes while foraging.

Slowly, scarcely daring to breathe, I leant forward to look around the bonnet of the car. I jumped back in shock and screamed. Something wearing a uniform with the garage brand on it had its face buried in the gaping bloody cavity of what had once been its poor victim's stomach. On hearing my scream, the creature raised its head. Its face, almost unrecognisable as that of a human being, was smeared with blood and it looked directly at me and snarled like a wildcat laying claim to its meal. Backing away, and almost falling over in my haste to get away, I stumbled back to my car.

Grabbing at the handle of the door, I yanked it open, threw myself into the seat and slammed the door again. Taking a few breaths to calm down, I turned to Becky and said shakily, "It's NOT a hoax!"

"What do you mean?" She was looking at me when Daisy let out a single high-pitched scream from the back.

The zombie had made its way over to our car and was standing behind it. It stared vacantly through the rear window, a piece of intestine still hanging from its mouth, which moved as it tried to chew and swallow it.

Daisy's scream attracted its attention and it made its way clumsily round the side of the car. Its shirt was blood soaked and shredded and I could see what looked like livid bite marks on its arms and body.

We sat glued to our seats and watched its progress. It was only when it lurched into the front of the car and stretched its arms over the bonnet in an attempt to reach us that the spell was broken and we all screamed in unison. At the sound of our screams it snarled again and began to claw at the car, its hands desperately but ineffectually trying to grip the smooth metal of the bonnet.

Snapping myself out of it I reached for the ignition, my hands shaking badly, and started the car.

I put the car into reverse, jammed my foot down on the accelerator and the car shot backwards, causing the zombie to fall face first on the ground. I slammed my foot on the brake and the car skidded to a stop just before it hit the boundary wall of the petrol station.

Looking back, to our horror, we saw it slowly pick itself up and start to stagger towards us again. I put the car in drive, and without looking at my mirrors, turned the wheel. With all four wheels spinning and tyres smoking, we shot back out on to the road.

"What the fuck is going on!" Becky screamed at me, "What was that?"

I came to, and realised that we were now travelling at over a hundred miles an hour.

Reluctantly, and with a glance at the rear-view mirror, I slowed the car down to a more respectable and safe eighty miles an hour.

The fact that both our kids were sobbing hysterically in the back of the car brought me fully back to my senses. I slowed the car down even more, hoping to find somewhere to stop in order to calm the children, Becky, and myself down.

When the speedometer dropped to twenty miles an hour, both Stanley and Daisy shrieked, "Don't stop, don't stop!"

"Stop the car NOW!" screamed Becky.

"It's ok, kids," I said soothingly, "Daddy's just going to stop the car. Nothing's going to happen to us. Look around, there's no one near us."

They kept looking nervously out of all the windows as I brought the car to a halt.

Becky sat quietly in her seat for a moment. Then she unclipped her seatbelt, leaned over and gave me a hug, and I hugged her back hard. She then disentangled herself from me and squeezing into the back of the car, hugged both of the kids together.

Once she was back in her seat she turned to me. "Are you going to tell me that we've landed in the middle of a zombie movie? Just tell me it's a dream."

"Darling, don't ask me how, but yes, if you like, we are in the middle of a zombie movie. No way was that normal back at the garage. The guy looked as if he'd been bitten himself; that must be how he got infected. What we don't know is how infectious they are. Will we turn into zomb-"

"Car!" shouted Stanley, who'd been watching out of the back window.

I looked in my wing mirror and saw the first car we'd seen on the roads all day, speeding towards us.

It was a BMW. It slowed down as it approached us and stopped about twenty feet away.

Grabbing the knife from the door pocket, I opened the door and got out.

A man stepped out of the car.

"Stop!" I shouted over to him, holding the knife out in front of me.

"What the hell is going on?" the man shouted back. "I've just seen someone being eaten by some maniac at the garage back there! When I tried to stop him, he tried to bite me!"

He walked towards me.

I waved the knife warily. "Stop! Don't come any closer!"

The man gestured hopelessly. "Why? What the fuck is going on? Why are you pointing a knife at me?" At this point it all got too much for him and he broke down.

I wavered slightly, feeling sorry for him. "Do you really have no idea what's going on?"

"No!" he said, wiping his eyes with his sleeve. "I've just spent the last few days walking a loop around south Cornwall. I mistimed my last walk, so I got back to the car too late to head home, and then spent the night in my car. This morning the weather was so nice I thought I'd walk a few more miles before heading home.

When I finished that, my first stop was at that petrol station. I still don't understand what I saw, but it scared the shit out of me and I drove off. Then I met you. Can you please just tell me what's going on?"

I thought for a moment, to compose my thoughts, before I spoke.

"Look," I said, feeling a little calmer, "We don't know much ourselves yet, but after all the reports this morning of people attacking each other, we decided to head for home. Now we've just heard a report that a virus is responsible. We must have seen the same zombie as you did at that garage. We stopped here to get our breath back."

The man looked at me in confusion. "Sorry. I thought you just said 'zombie'?"

"Yes, pal," I replied patiently. "Somehow we appear to be right in the middle of a zombie apocalypse. And please don't take this the wrong way, but you've been in close contact with one. I don't know how it spreads, so I don't want you any closer to me or my family than you already are. I just can't take the risk."

To my surprise, his demeanour changed. He stood straighter and a determined look came into his eyes. He looked at me thoughtfully for a minute or so, and then spoke up. "Are you serious? I've hardly seen anyone and I certainly haven't spoken to anyone since I started my walk. I prefer to choose the more out-of-the-way footpaths."

I nodded, "Ok, but you just said you got close to the zombie at the garage. Look, I don't really know. But I think if I'm going to be able to protect my family, it's best to assume the worst and believe that somehow the impossible has happened."

We all turned as we heard the sound of another car approaching. This time it was a Range Rover. It was also travelling at breakneck speed and as it got closer it pulled into the other lane to overtake us. It slowed slightly as it passed, and I saw a wild-eyed man and woman staring out at us. It had tinted windows, so I couldn't see if there was anyone in the back.

They seemed to come to a decision because the car suddenly screeched to a halt and reversed back towards us. The woman wound down her window and shouted,

"Where's the hospital? My kids have both been bitten by someone and they need help!"

The man and I both took a step back.

Increasingly desperate now, she said, "Please! They're unconscious. I have to get my babies to a hospital."

The man interrupted her. "He's waking up!" He jumped out of the car, opened the rear door and lifted out a boy of about twelve, then stood there holding him, helplessly. He was on the other side of the car so my view was restricted, but I could see the boy lying motionless in his arms.

The man looked down as the boy's arms started to twitch. "He's coming round," he said, sounding relieved. "His eyes are moving."

I knew what was about to happen, but I couldn't say a word. It couldn't happen! This was not a movie.

The child in the man's arms jerked his head upwards and wrapped his arms around his father's neck.

"It's ok, Henry," the man said, "Dad's he… aarrrggh," was all he managed to say, before his son bit deeply into his neck. He must have bitten straight through his windpipe and vocal cords, because his father's scream turned into a wet gurgle, and he barely made a sound as he fell out of sight behind the car.

We all screamed again in horror. The woman shrieking for someone to help her from the front of the car. As we watched, a little girl's head appeared from the back. Arms outstretched, as if seeking comfort, she crawled slowly over to her mother, who turned towards her instinctively.

The little girl growled and sank her teeth into her mother's cheek. The woman's shrieks turned to squeals of pain.

I turned my head away and came to a decision. We had to look after our kids. We needed to get away.

I could hear Becky, Stanley and Daisy moaning and weeping at what they were witnessing. I turned to the man and shouted at him, "We're off. Try to stay away from everyone until you find out more. Good luck mate."

He seemed to have completely regained his composure. "I'm heading to the moors. I've got some food but I'm pretty good at foraging. If this is 'the zombie apocalypse' it's one of the things I'm prepared for. My 'Bug-Out' bag is in the boot of my car and I've got some goodies hidden away in the car for an event like this."

I was about to step into the car when he said this, so I stopped and looked at him. "Your Bug-Out what? Why do you suddenly look better to me?"

Raising his voice over the sound of the screaming woman in the car, he continued. "I'm a prepper, mate. There are a lot of us around and we've spent years talking about and preparing for various events.

We normally talk about the possibility of a zombie apocalypse for fun! But we're prepped for it all the same. As far as I'm concerned, I've survived the outbreak and now I'm going to escape, evade and survive. It's why I've spent weeks walking in the countryside. I've been practising my skills for when I need them."

Sheepishly, he added, "Sorry about breaking down just now and screaming like a girl. I guess it was just the shock. Anyway, as I was saying, I always keep a rucksack in my car full of all the things I'll need. I call it my bug-out bag. It'll help me survive wherever I go."

I thought quickly, "If you're the expert now, what should we do?"

He stopped and considered my question for a moment and then spoke. "You were on the right track when you said we need to stay away from people until we can understand what's caused it. It's all about survival now. Gather food when and where you can. Only eat foraged food that you're familiar with; some of the things that grow in the wild can kill you. Being part of a group is better in terms of protection, but you must trust each other or it won't work."

He paused for breath then carried on, "It's all down to common sense, really. Try to find out what attracts the zombies and try not to do it. We all believe that the best way to kill a zombie is to destroy the brain.

It would be best to test that theory out in a controlled environment to start with if you can, because your life will depend on knowing how to kill one."

He looked round at the Range Rover. The woman had stopped screaming and was either dead or unconscious. Her daughter was still feeding greedily on her face and neck.

"In fact…," he walked calmly round to the boot of his car and leant in. He rummaged for a few seconds and emerged holding a large knife. He removed it from its sheath. It was about ten inches long with a sharp point and looked wickedly sharp on one edge. The other edge was serrated. He walked deliberately over to the open window of the Range Rover.

The little girl took no notice of him and was occupied with tearing off chunks of her mother's flesh. He grabbed her by the hair, and before I could say anything, drove the knife deeply into her head. She slumped forward, dead.

He wiped his knife on the mother's shirt and put the knife back in its sheath.

Then he bent over, retched violently and threw up. A lot. I waited a minute or two for him to recover. "Sorry," he said, wiping his mouth with a handkerchief from his pocket. "I had to get that over with before I had time to think about what I was going to do.

I think we can now confirm that a zombie can be killed by a knife through the brain."

He pointed at Becky, Stanley and Daisy, who were staring open mouthed out of the window of the car, and continued. "Sorry about doing it in front of your family, but I suppose they'll need to get used to it at some point."

I was unable to speak, so I just waved my hands around like an idiot.

A noise reached us from behind the Range Rover, and the son stood up and started to move, arms reaching out towards us in a classic zombie pose.

Without thinking, I said, "I've got this one."

Absolutely shitting myself, I walked towards him with my carving knife held out in front of me. I thrust the knife towards his face but the blade sliced deeply through his nose and then just glanced off. He didn't even flinch. As I stepped back and he advanced, I must have looked terrified. Hands trembling, I tried to stab him in the side of the head, but the cheap thin blade didn't penetrate far enough.

It would have caused a debilitating injury to a normal human being, but instead it just bent against his skull and deformed the blade. Holding my now useless blade in my hand, I tried to turn and run, but the boy's outstretched hand caught my shoulder and his fingers closed around my shirt. Losing it completely, I let out a yell of fright. The thought flashed across my mind that I was going to be eaten by a zombie and die.

A second thought followed swiftly afterwards, *"What a dickhead, I'm only going to survive the first half hour of an apocalypse!"*

As if in a dream, I saw the zombie's head jerk back and watched as a knife was thrust in and pulled out again. It collapsed and lay motionless on the road. I staggered back and fell against the car, my legs like warm jelly. As my senses began to return and I became aware of my surroundings, I heard my family in the car, screaming and crying again. I looked up at my saviour, who was standing with his survival knife still in his hand, blood dripping from its blade.

"Thanks," I croaked.

Reassuringly, the man replied, "Don't worry about it. You had him on the first thrust. It was your knife that let you down."

"I almost got bitten on my first attempt at killing one and you're telling me not to worry!" I said despairingly. "That was my best knife and it's fucking useless."

He walked over to me. I forgot all about my fears about him being contagious, and we shook hands.

"Bollocks! It's a bit late to worry about you being infected now," I said, remembering.

All I heard from the car was, "Tom, stop swearing. It's bad enough as it is."

I raised my eyebrows at the man in resignation and he grinned.

"Tom, I know you're pulling a face!" came the next complaint through the car window.

We smiled and it helped to calm us both down. Then we started to chuckle, and before long we were actually giggling.

I guess it was the relief. I realised that the kids had stopped crying and were just sitting there, staring at me.

Amazing really, considering that in a short space of time they had witnessed two people being attacked, bitten and killed, their attackers being dispatched by a knife into their brains, and their father almost being bitten in the process.

Maybe today's video games had desensitized them.

Chapter nine

"Can we start again?" I said to the man. "I'm Tom and that's my wife Becky, and those are my kids, Stanley and Daisy, in the back."

He waved his hand at them in greeting. "Shawn Graveling." He looked around and frowned. "Where is everyone? This is normally a busy road."

"Not a clue. The radio told everyone to stay indoors and avoid contact with other people. Maybe they're all doing that."

"Come on. Some people might be, but you didn't. There should be loads of people trying to get home, just like you. This road should be like a racetrack. It's the main summer season, there are thousands of holidaymakers in tents or caravans, and they must all be starting to realise that they're not safe and they need to head for home."

"We were in a caravan; that's why we decided to go."

"Exactly. So where are the rest of them?"

As if in response to his question, we heard an explosion in the distance. Looking towards St Agnes, we could see a huge column of smoke rising.

"Perhaps that's why," said Shawn, looking troubled. "However this thing is spreading, it looks as if you might have got out of Dodge just in time. It doesn't look good in that direction."

~

v'd had a bird's eye view over St Agnes, they would
d scenes of chaos. The infection had been carried
e traveller, a lad of twenty, returning from a six-
in.

Vladimir had walked past him, coughing while he'd been waiting for his rucksack to arrive at Heathrow Airport.

Having cleared Customs, he'd set out on the long coach ride home to see his family in St Agnes, passing the virus on to other passengers on the coach, all of whom disembarked at stops throughout the West Country.

Having arrived home late and enjoyed a quick catch up with his family, he'd met up with his friends and they'd embarked on a pub crawl to celebrate his homecoming. By the time he'd staggered home in the early hours of the morning, feeling decidedly worse for wear, a good portion of the small Cornish village had been exposed to the infection. He was destined never to know this.

When his parents, both beginning to feel off colour themselves, walked into the room he shared with his six year-old brother the following morning, they found a blood-streaked ghoul feasting on what was left of the little boy's body.

As the number of zombies increased, the trickle of people who had heard the news and had decided to make for home quickly turned into a flood. Many of them would have made it too, had it not been for one man's mistake. In his panic to get out, a tourist had tried to overtake a slower moving car on a bend and had collided head-on with a lorry, effectively blocking the main route out of the village.

The explosion and smoke Tom and Shawn saw were the result of a spark igniting the leaking fuel from the crashed car, and setting off a chain reaction, culminating in a fuel lorry, caught in the traffic jam and unable to move, exploding as soon as the flames reached it.

From then on, most people, still not fully aware of the magnitude of the situation, became easy prey for the zombies.

Even the people who managed to escape initially, came into contact with those who were infected when they tried to seek shelter. The Darwinian process had begun.

If you learned quickly, and were able to adapt, you might just stand a chance of surviving. If you weren't able to do that, well it was just a matter of time.

One mistake would end in you and your family dying, or worse, becoming one of the legions of zombies who were now roaming the earth, looking for their next meal. Most people, sadly, fell into the latter category.

The picture was a similar one the world over. Most countries were experiencing outbreaks of the virus. Some countries had some initial success in controlling the spread, but didn't take action quickly enough to close their borders. As a result, many people fled in panic, making the problem worse.

Island nations had a geographical advantage, and could have isolated themselves until the infectious cold-based stage of the virus had run its course on the mainland. Most, though, failed to do this. As Tom and Shawn stood in the middle of the road, staring at the ominous cloud of smoke, all of this was irrelevant. The only thing they were certain of was that the little part of England they were standing in was going to shit.

~

We stood there quietly for a moment until Becky shouted, "Tom! What on earth are you doing?" and snapped me out of it.

I turned and was about to wish Shawn good luck before we went our separate ways, when he passed me the knife he was holding, saying, "Please take it. I have others and you've got your family to protect."

I was about to thank him when I heard another car approaching, this time from the other direction, the way I was intending to go; towards the A30 and home.

Again, this car was travelling at breakneck speed, but it started to slow down as it approached us. It was a Mercedes saloon and as it got closer, the driver's window began to open. We both stepped back and I gripped my new knife tightly. We could see a man and a woman in the front and two teenagers in the back. They all looked scared to death.

"You need to turn around and get out of here!" he screamed at us.

In his agitated state, it was difficult to understand exactly what he was saying but I heard something along the lines of: "It's like the news this morning! People are eating each other! The main road's blocked; we can't go that way …" Then he spotted the body of the man from the Range Rover, sprawled beside his car with his throat a gaping mess of chewed flesh, and his son lying on the road with his brains spilling out of the wound Shawn had inflicted. On top of everything he'd already experienced, this seemed to push him over the edge.

He screamed and slammed the car into gear. Realising that he was heading in the direction of the explosion, I ran forward and shouted for him to stop. In his desperation he either couldn't, or didn't want to hear me, and with his engine over-revving and his tyres screeching, he sped away towards St Agnes, and the rising smoke. He was driving far too fast and was struggling to control the car, which was fishtailing down the road. He clearly wasn't used to driving at speed, and kept overcorrecting as the car's rear end swung from side to side in an increasingly erratic way. The rear wheel of the Mercedes hit the kerb and he lost control completely.

The car shot across the carriageway, and we heard the engine screaming in protest as the man kept his foot down hard on the accelerator. The vehicle slammed into the other kerb, flipped over and flew through the air. Then it rolled and virtually disintegrated as it smashed through a wall.

We watched in shocked silence as what was left of the car continued to roll down a bank into a field and disappeared from view. I hadn't heard Becky get out of the car, so when she spoke beside me, I jumped. "What are we going to do now?" she asked, looking white. "That man said the main road's blocked. And whatever he's seen scared him enough to drive like that," she said, pointing at the trail of destruction.

Shawn spoke up, "As I said, I'm heading off to the moors to get out of the way."

"How are you going to get there?" asked Becky, remarkably calm, considering what we'd all experienced in the last five minutes. "Bodmin Moor's quite a way from here, and if everyone's driving like that bloke, you certainly don't want to be on the roads. And he said the main road's going to be blocked anyway!"

Shawn nodded and stood there looking thoughtful. I walked over to the car and opened the rear door to reassure Stanley and Daisy. They threw themselves at me, and I hugged them both tightly, telling them over and over that it was all going to be ok.

Mommy and Daddy would work something out.

Shawn had an Ordnance Survey map spread out on the bonnet of the car. It was the 1:25000 scale map of the area and was much more detailed than the usual road map.

Becky joined us for a family hug and stayed to comfort the kids while Shawn and I traced a route with our fingers that would use the back roads and avoid as many villages and hamlets as possible.

Looking up at me, he said, "You know what, I think I'd be happier if we travelled together. Being on your own is all very well in theory, but if we join forces, at least in the short term, we'll be able to help each other out."

Unable to see a downside and feeling secretly relieved, I agreed. He was a prepper and knew things that I didn't about living in the wild. As he'd already said, a zombie apocalypse was one of the things they were ready for.

My sole responsibility was my family's safety and welfare and at that precise moment, as far as I was concerned, Shawn could play a big part in keeping us alive.

Becky shouted, "Tom, look!" and we both swung round and looked in the direction she was pointing.

Chapter ten

The woman in the front of the Range Rover was moving, her head jerking from side to side. A cold feeling of dread came over me.

"I thought she was dead!" I shouted.

"What's it been? No more than ten minutes, and she's turned," said Shawn, thoughtfully. "This is straight out of the Zombie Instruction Manual! We need to know what we're dealing with here, Tom. If you could get Becky to move the kids to the other side of the car, I think we need to do a bit of research."

"What do you mean, research?" I asked, confused.

He looked at me sharply, placed his hand on my shoulder and then said slowly and clearly, as if addressing a child, "Tom, I'm going to get another knife and then we'll see exactly what kind of zombies we're dealing with. In the meantime, I don't think you're going to want your kids to see what I'm going to do."

Becky, always quicker on the uptake, had been listening and nodded. She threw me a look of sympathy and led the kids around to the other side of the car. My instincts were telling me to get as far away from the place as possible, but Shawn was completely calm and collected.

Once he'd understood what was happening, his whole personality seemed to have changed and he was acting as if being in the middle of a zombie apocalypse was an everyday occurrence.

All business now, Shawn walked briskly to the boot of his car and came back with a similar looking knife to the one he'd given me. Stepping over the body of her son, we gingerly approached the woman.

She looked as if she was waking from a deep sleep. Her movements were spasmodic and uncoordinated, her eyes opening and closing but not focusing on anything.

"Is she alive?" I whispered.

"She's been bitten, which according to zombie folklore means she's been infected," Shawn whispered back.

"Her movements aren't normal so I would say no, she's not alive. She's in the first stage of becoming a zombie."

"I can't believe we're talking like this," I said, shaking my head, "Have you heard yourself?"

Shawn turned, walked back to his open boot and came back with a short length of rope.

"What are you doing now?"

"I'm going to tie her up some more," he replied. "Her seatbelt won't keep her still enough and I for one am not going to take the chance of getting bitten."

Opening the rear of the car, Shawn gently pulled the little girl out and laid her respectfully on the road. Watching him do this brought me fully back to myself, and realising that I needed to help, I stepped forward.

We worked together to secure the woman's head to the headrest and made sure her arms were immobilised so that she wouldn't be able to grab us. As we were doing this, her movements became more coordinated and low groaning sounds were emitting from her throat.

The sound sent a chill through me.

As we stood back to admire our handiwork, we were startled by the sound of a car hurtling by at top speed. Our attention had been focused on tying the woman up, so we hadn't heard it approach.

We couldn't see how many people were in the car, but the brief glimpse we got showed that most of its body panels were bashed and scraped, and the rear bumper was dragging along behind it.

"No wonder we haven't seen any other cars," I remarked, watching it disappear into the distance. "If that's the state of the one that got out, it must be bloody awful there."

Shawn made no comment. He looked back at the woman and said, "I think we can safely say that's a zombie."

We stepped closer for a better look, knives raised, just in case.

The woman's complexion was grey and mottled, and her eyes were dull and blank, open but still unfocused. The groaning increased and she gnashed her teeth together.

Sensing our approach, she tried to turn her head towards us but the ropes held her secure. Her groans grew louder and turned to snarls, and her movements became more agitated and desperate as she tried to struggle free.

Involuntarily, we stepped back, then stood in silence and watched her for a while.

She was breathing like an asthmatic smoker, her breaths laboured and noisy like a death rattle.

"She's breathing!" I exclaimed, "Zombies aren't meant to do that, are they?"

Shawn nodded, "Well that's settled zombie argument number one. I always thought it was wrong that zombies were portrayed as not needing to breathe, meaning that they could stay underwater, or be buried and then come out and attack people. They're still an organic lifeform, after all, so I guess they need oxygen to survive. That's good news for us."

"Why?" I asked, not quite feeling up to "prepper level" in terms of understanding zombies.

"We can use it as another way to kill them, and deep water will keep us safe."

I nodded, trying hard to understand what he was getting at.

"It should also mean," he continued enthusiastically, "that they need to eat to survive. That's good news, because eventually, easy food sources will run out and they should start to die off through starvation. And before you say anything, I haven't got a clue how long that will take."

Looking meaningfully at me, he said, "Now just keep telling yourself that this is not a human being."

He stabbed his knife into the woman's leg. She gave no visible signs of pain. He then stabbed her repeatedly in the arms and chest.

He stood back and watched her. She'd been stabbed enough times to kill her, but the only sign of distress she showed was a redoubling of her efforts to escape her bonds.

I noted with a sick feeling that her lungs had been pierced and a small amount of dark frothy blood was bubbling around the puncture wounds.

"She's not bleeding much," observed Shawn, for all the world as if we were in a lecture. "Now if this had been a normal person you'd expect to see gallons of blood pouring out." I now began to understand the reason for his gory experiment. The knowledge we were gaining would enable us to dispatch them more easily when it became necessary.

Shawn was clearly getting into his stride. "There must be a reason why they bleed so little, but for our purposes I guess all we need to know is that the only sure fire way to kill one is to destroy the brain, either by bashing their skulls in, or removing their heads.

Or maybe suffocating them. I suspect taking the heart out would do it too but that'd be a bit tricky to carry off first time."

"Now let's see how they hunt." He went back to his car, and after more rummaging, returned with a small red towel and a tent pole.

I looked at him quizzically, as he tied the towel to the end of the pole.

Quietly, he made his way back to the car, holding the pole out in front of him. The zombie stopped thrashing about as the towel was dangled about six feet in front of it. As Shawn moved it, her eyes followed the red towel.

Placing the pole carefully down on the bonnet, he approached the car as quietly as possible. Then he suddenly clapped his hands together loudly near her head. Her eyes reacted instantly, swivelling towards the sound. It was clear that she would also have turned her head had it not been securely tied to the headrest.

"Ok," said Shawn slowly, "That's not such good news. They can see and hear; I'm not sure just how well yet, but we'll assume they can do both brilliantly until it's proved otherwise. It won't do any harm."

Becky shouted suddenly, "I can see something moving!" and we spun round to look. "Stanley spotted it as we were playing I spy," she explained.

I reached into the front of my car and removed the pair of compact binoculars I kept in the glove box. Lifting them to my eyes, it only took a few seconds to get them into focus.

"I think we need to get moving," I said, as I handed the binoculars to Shawn.

About twenty zombies were heading our way along the road from St Agnes.

"Surely we need to help him, though?" asked Shawn.

"Who?" I asked.

"The child they're hunting," he said, handing the binoculars back.

I looked again and saw with a jolt that a young boy of about ten was running flat out about twenty metres ahead of the zombies. As I continued to watch, the gap started to widen, but then he stopped and looked around uncertainly, as if unsure about where to go. It was only when they started to get closer that he started running again. Now that he was nearer to us I could see the look of abject terror on his face.

"What is it?" asked Becky, trying to snatch at the binoculars.

"Zombies. Chasing a young boy," I said, knowing exactly what her next words were going to be.

"You need to go and rescue him! NOW!" she shouted.

I looked at Shawn. He nodded grimly. "Let's take my car."

I turned to Becky, "Lock yourself in the car, darling. If anything happens to me, just drive."

Becky nodded, unable to speak, and the children, realising that I was about to head into danger again, started to cry quietly.

"Put your thickest coat on for protection," said Shawn, pulling on a heavy duty waterproof jacket.

As I opened the boot of my car, he noticed the cricket bat sitting on top of the pile. Without hesitation, he walked over and grabbed it. "I think we might need this," was all he said.

I snatched up my leather jacket and hurriedly put it on.

With no more time to waste, we jumped into Shawn's car and sped off towards the boy and the zombies.

"How do we do this?" I asked, trying not to sound nervous.

Shawn shrugged. "Fuck knows. I'll stop next to him, you grab him and if any zombies get close we'll either use the cricket bat or we'll knife them in the head. Does that sound like a plan?" He looked at me and I shrugged in my turn.

"I suppose."

We were only fifty metres away from the boy, but he'd stopped running when he'd seen us approaching. "Shit!" I yelled. "They're getting too close to him. We need to do something!"

Shawn drove his car towards the boy, and at the very last minute, flicked the wheel and pulled the handbrake on. He executed a perfect handbrake turn.

In response, the rear of the car spun around and smashed into the two zombies that were closest to the boy. The car was now between the zombies and the boy, and pointing back to where we wanted to go.

I turned and looked at him, lost for words.

"I didn't know if that was going to work," he replied modestly.

Opening the door with a shove, I jumped out of the car and ran towards the boy. He was just standing there, tears streaming down his dirt-streaked face, trembling with shock and fear. With no time for niceties, I picked him up and raced back to the car.

It was only when I tried to push him into the car that I realised my mistake. Shawn's car was only a three door so there was no rear door for me to use. I glanced up to see a zombie just six feet away from me and getting closer all the time. I almost turned and ran at the sight of it. It was hideously burned and must either have been caught in the fire we'd seen or just walked heedlessly through it.

What was left of its clothes was still smouldering and all the flesh I could see was either charred or burned away completely, with white bone showing in places. The creature was like something out of a nightmare and it was heading straight for me.

With a massive effort, I resisted the urge to run and took a step towards it. The knife was still in my hand and with a downwards stroke I rammed it into the top of its skull. It began to fall towards me, and filled with revulsion, I kicked out with my foot and shoved it away from me. Luckily, it fell backwards into the zombie behind it. Seizing my chance, I dived on to the passenger seat with the boy and screamed, "GO!"

Shawn put his foot down and the car sped back up the road, with my feet sticking out of the open door.

Seconds later, the car slowed and Shawn said simply, "Well done mate, now let's get out of here."

Chapter eleven

I looked up and realised that we were back at my car. Becky had got out and was running over to us. I managed to push myself upright and lifted myself off the boy, who was looking pale and shocked. He gave no reaction but just sat and stared straight ahead. Becky enveloped me in a hug.

"We need to make sure he hasn't been bitten," said Shawn, climbing out of the car. "And we definitely need to go now," he said, pointing down the road at the horde of zombies, who were still making steady progress.

As I leant into the car to pull the boy out, Becky pulled on my arm to stop me. "No," she said quietly. "Let me do it."

I stood back and Becky crouched down in the car doorway. I couldn't hear what she was saying, but within seconds she'd managed to snap him out of his trance-like state and he'd got himself out of the car.

Becky knelt next to him and gave him a motherly hug.

"Shit!" I said quietly to Shawn, "He might be infected. I never even thought. We could all have it now."

"Bollocks!" he muttered. "I didn't think about it either. Oh well," he shrugged, "It's too late now, but we'll need to be more careful next time. I've got some surgical masks in my bug-out bag for this very eventuality." Noting my distress, he shook his head and chuckled, adding, "I'm the bloody prepper, mate. I should know all this and I still forgot. Don't be so hard on yourself. If we get away with it, and he's not infected, then at least we'll have learnt a valuable lesson!"

I nodded. "Where shall we go?"

"Right, this is the best plan I've been able to come up with in the short time we've had, so please feel free to add suggestions or correct me if you want.

I think you should lead the way in your car, because it's bigger than mine, and we might have to use it as a battering ram, if there are any obstacles along the way.

It'll also stand up to knocking zombies over better than my car. We'll try following the route we mapped out. If that route turns out to be blocked, we'll have to start making it up, but if we remain vigilant and stay away from the bigger population centres, we might be able to avoid the infected areas. I've studied how viruses spread as part of my prepping, and it can't have got everywhere this quickly."

"Why not?"

He smiled wryly and said, "Well we ain't got it for a start. So that probably rules out an airborne infection. It's most likely being passed by physical contact, or contact with people in very close proximity, so that's why we should use the surgical masks for the time being."

The zombies were still about two hundred metres away. In fairness, this was still a hundred miles closer than any of us wanted them to be.

"Let's get going," I said hastily.

While we'd been talking, Becky had put the boy in the back of the car and he was sitting quietly between Stanley and Daisy. She walked over to us. "He hasn't been bitten, and he says he didn't see anyone until the bad people hurt his parents and he ran away. I don't think he's been infected."

Once more Shawn went to the boot of his car. He came back with another knife, some surgical masks and a two-way radio. "The knife's for you, Becky, just in case, and I've got the other radio so that we can talk. The left turn's just around the bend, so keep checking your mirrors even though I should be right behind you."

He pressed the call buttons on the radios to make sure they were both on the same channel, and passed the radio and knife over to me. "We'll put the masks on if we meet anyone else until we know for sure that they're not infected. It's not worth taking any risks."

With no time to waste, as the zombies were getting closer all the time, we set off in the cars.

Once we were moving, Stanley and Daisy started asking questions again. Becky turned to them and said carefully, "Listen to me, both of you. Mommy and Daddy need you to be very brave. Something's turning people nasty and we need to get away from them. You mustn't worry; you saw what a hero Daddy was when he rescued Eddie. He won't let anything happen to us. Now you need to be really quiet and let us concentrate so that we can find somewhere safe."

I glanced in my rear-view mirror and saw that Shawn was right behind us. Then I looked at the faces of my two beautiful kids, filled with terror but trying hard to control their emotions. Finally, I looked at Eddie, who was still looking too shocked to take anything in. He was a stocky lad, probably about Stanley's age, with a mass of straight ginger hair which stuck up in places. His grubby, tear stained face was covered in freckles.

"Who could blame him", I thought. *"He's almost certainly seen his parents being eaten alive and only barely escaped himself, and he's been hunted by a pack of zombies."*

"Hi Eddie," I said gently. "My name's Tom. How old are you?"

There was a long pause. "Ten," came the monosyllabic response.

All a bit much for your average ten-year-old to take in really, I thought. Oh well, looks like we have a new addition to the family.

I slowed down as the turning came up and we headed down a narrow single-track road. I zoomed the map out on the sat nav so that I could get an idea of where we were and the direction we needed to take. We'd come down this road a few days before, looking for a pub recommended on Trip Advisor, so parts of it were familiar to me.

As we rounded a corner I slammed the brakes on. A farm trailer was parked across the road, blocking our way completely. Shawn must have been on the alert because he managed to skid to a halt without hitting me.

I sat there for a moment, gathering my shattered nerves back together.

I could see someone moving on the other side of the trailer, so I quickly donned my mask and made everyone else do the same. Then I stepped out of the car, my knife at my side in readiness. Before I closed the door, I warned Becky to keep a look out and to shout if she saw anything.

Shawn, wearing his mask, joined me.

"Hello! Is anyone there?" I shouted.

"Go away!" came the response. "We're not letting anyone through. For all we know you might be one of the terrorists."

Shawn and I exchanged amused glances. "What do you mean, terrorists?" I asked with incredulity.

A man came out into the open. He looked like a typical farmer and was wearing the standard boiler suit with a checked shirt underneath and green wellies on his feet. Nothing out of the ordinary, apart from the shotgun he was carrying.

"We've heard about the attacks in town," he said, his face hostile. "And we've seen the fires they've started. We don't want any of that element coming here, so we've blocked the roads. There are no police close by so we've taken steps to protect ourselves."

I stepped forward. "But you've got it all wrong; we're trying to get away." I pointed at my car, "Look, I've got my wife and kids with me and another boy we've just rescued. Shawn here's with us. We're helping each other."

The man gave no response. "It's not terrorists," I persisted, "It's zombies that are attacking. There are people turning into zombies and they're ripping other people apart and eating them. Don't ask me how, or why, but we need to keep going. The main road's blocked and they'll be heading this way soon."

"Please!" said Shawn, "You have to believe us. They'll be here soon!"

More people had appeared while I'd been talking and had been listening to what we'd been saying. Some of them also carried shotguns and one had a rifle.

The farmer shook his head and laughed. "How do you expect us to believe that? That's ridiculous! You're just making it up to try to get us to let you through. God alone knows what would happen then!"

Behind me I heard a car door open and close, and I turned to see Becky walking towards us.

"You need to listen to my husband," she said, her voice pleading. "It's not terrorists or anything like that. I know it doesn't sound credible, but there *are* zombies. We've already been attacked and we've just had to rescue that little boy back there. Back on the main road we all watched another young boy kill his father by biting into his neck. We found the assistant at the petrol station feeding on one of the customers. You're right to want to protect yourselves, but please, you need to let us through. I need to get my children somewhere safe. If you don't believe us, just go back up to the main road and see for yourself. But be careful. Don't go near any of them."

They all turned and talked among themselves for a minute. The farmer turned back to us, "All right. We'll go and have a look. Why are you wearing masks?"

While I was explaining, the trailer was hauled out of the way by a tractor. A man and a woman on a quad bike squeezed through the gap and roared up the road.

I realised that I'd been clutching my knife tightly throughout, and put it back into its sheath, which I'd clipped onto my belt. As I did so, I noticed everyone relaxing slightly.

"Sorry," I said. "Forgot I was still holding it. It's been a hell of a day!"

In less than a minute, we heard the quad bike returning. As expected, it was travelling much faster than it had done on the way out. It skidded to a halt right beside us.

"Fucking zombies!" the man yelled. "They tried to get us, but we turned around just in time. Jim Barker was one of them. He was covered in blood and half his arm was hanging off, but he still tried to grab me!"

Everyone started shouting at once until the farmer finally had to bawl at them all to be quiet. He turned to us.

"So it's like 'The Walking Dead'?"

"Yes," Shawn, Becky and I said together.

He released a few mouthfuls of expletives before turning to us again.

"What can we do?"

Shawn seized his opportunity. "Well, believe it or not, this is something I've prepared for. First you need to let us through, then you have two choices. Stay or go, it's as simple as that. If you stay here, you'll need to work together. Build barriers and fences; anything to stop them or at least slow them down.

You can only kill them by destroying their brains so prepare yourselves for that, and gather what weapons you have. I notice you have shotguns and rifles. Great! But conserve your cartridges and ammunition because once you've run out you'll be in trouble.

We've found out by tying one up and experimenting, that they need to breathe, but as I've said, the best way to kill them is to target the brain.

I don't know how many you'll be facing, but we've only seen one car leave St Agnes and that looked as if it had to fight its way out. There could be thousands of the things heading your way. You've seen the fictional version, now you're going to be living it. Oh, and we know they can see reasonably well and are attracted to noise, so bear that in mind."

He paused to let it all sink in. The farmer turned to the couple on the quadbike, "How many were there?"

"Twenty or so," replied the woman, "I didn't stop to count them!"

"First of all, we need to get everyone together. They all need to know exactly what's happening." He turned to us. "Sorry about not letting you through before. You might just have saved all our lives. Is there anything we can do to help you before you go?"

I shrugged, not really knowing what to say, but Shawn replied without hesitation. "Some water would be useful, or at least a container I can carry some in. I only have my water bottle and there are more of us now." He paused for a moment, thinking. "A tarpaulin would be good too, and maybe some better weapons. And if you could spare any tinned food, that would be great."

"I'm sure we can sort most of that out," he said. "Do you want to come with me?"

He pointed to a farm building about a hundred metres away. "Just let me speak to the rest of the village first."

He gave orders for the trailer to be moved and we pulled forward, thankful for the protection it offered.

While the farmer was waiting for everyone to gather, we took the chance to get the kids out of the car.

There are only so many "it's going to be all rights" you can say when you're in the middle of a zombie apocalypse.

Stanley, who had always been very perceptive, and quick to assess any situation he was in, summed it up,

"Dad. Those people we saw are dead, aren't they? If we don't kill them, they'll kill us, so you need to show me how to do it. If something happens to you, then I can still protect Mommy and Daisy."

The way he stood there, looking so small, but trying so hard to be the man he wanted to be, brought tears to my eyes. I gave him a fierce hug. "Stanley, from now on I'm going to need your help. I can't make things any easier, but we probably will have to do and see some truly awful things. Things nobody should ever have to deal with. I'm relying on you to be my right-hand man."

He stood even straighter and seemed to grow a few inches in height, "What about Eddie, Dad, can he help as well?"

I looked over at Eddie. The poor kid was still traumatised but clearly yearned for approval.

"Of course! I'm going to need both of you. You look like a strong lad, Eddie. Do you think you could help us?"

Eddie looked at me and his face changed slightly. The haunted look started to fade and was replaced by a look of determination. He suddenly seemed more aware of his surroundings. I couldn't help but wonder how many more people we would have to gather to us before this was all over.

The sound of a gunshot and a scream of "zombies!" made me pull my knife back out of my sheath. Grabbing the children, I got them back to the safest place I could think of: my car.

I saw Shawn reaching for Stanley's cricket bat and stopped him, saying, "Can I have that back please? I think I know someone who wants it."

Becky was standing by the car with her knife in her hands. I opened the car and handed Stanley the cricket bat.

Hunkering down, I looked at him and said, "I need you to have this, son. If they get too close, just hit them as hard as you can until they fall over."

He grabbed it and nodded fiercely.

I ran back to the trailer. I could see that there were at least twenty zombies approaching. It looked like the same group we'd rescued Eddie from. I actually recognised a few of them; presumably they'd followed the quad bike back, proving the theory that they were attracted by sight and sound. They probably just kept on going, doggedly pursuing whatever caught their attention, until distracted by something else.

"Aim for the head!" I yelled, as I could see that, despite a few shots being fired, none of the zombies were down.

The man with the rifle took aim and fired but as far as I could tell, completely missed. Minute by minute they were getting closer. Someone else fired his shotgun and hit the nearest zombie in the arm.

The arm hung gruesomely from the elbow by a scrap of skin but, undaunted, the thing kept coming.

Already feeling like a veteran, I looked at Shawn and said, "Shall we?"

He nodded.

I shouted, "Stop firing!" over and over as we stepped past the trailer and stood facing the crowd of flesh hungry zombies.

I wasn't thinking about the villagers. My wife and my children were behind the barricade and if any of them got any closer, there was a chance they could get through. I needed to stop them now.

I lunged at the nearest zombie, stabbed it through the top of its head and pushed it away. I went for the next and rammed my knife through the side of its head. Much better; the blade passed smoothly in and out.

"Stab them through the side; it's easier!" I shouted to Shawn, who I could see out of the corner of my eye, was attacking those closest to him. The zombies had spaced themselves out nicely, rather than bunching up. Very thoughtful of them, because it made our job much simpler.

Stab push, stab push.

It wasn't long before we'd killed them all. When there were no more left, it took a few seconds for us both to realise that it was over. Panting with a mixture of terror and exertion and dripping with sweat, we gazed in shock at our handiwork.

The ground in front of the barricade was littered with crumpled bodies. The sound of cheers and clapping brought us out of our reverie. The sheer raw excitement and exhilaration of what we'd done hit us both. We'd just taken part in a mad stabbing frenzy and slaughtered over twenty zombies. We'd faced up to one of the most frightening things imaginable and come out of it successfully.

We were zombie killers. We were going to survive this!

We shouted and punched the air, primal emotions building up inside us. The villagers surrounded us, strangers we'd never met before congratulating us, grabbing our hands, and thanking us for saving their lives.

I looked down at myself and then looked at Shawn, surprised that we weren't covered in more blood. Yes, we'd been splattered with some when it had sprayed off our knife blades, but unlike in the movies where you couldn't kill a zombie without being coated from head to toe in blood and gore, the truth was that zombies don't bleed much.

Perhaps it was the fact that their metabolism was slower. Their heart rate and blood pressure were likely to be much reduced, as they only needed to move to get to the next meal and weren't performing any of the highly complex tasks normally required of our bodies, tasks which tend to require substantial amounts of energy.

With the help of the world's most powerful computers, scientists were just beginning to build humanoid robots capable of successfully replicating simple movements. Our remarkable bodies accomplish complex tasks using their matrix of brain power, muscles, tendons and senses, all of which enable us to balance from when we are about one year old, but that expends a lot of energy. A zombie didn't need all those abilities, so it made sense that their bodies slowed down to conserve energy.

Chapter twelve

As I walked back behind the trailer, Becky hurled herself at me again. I hadn't been hugged that much for ages. In fact, if it hadn't been for the zombie situation I'd have suspected her of being after something.

I pushed her away gently. "Let's get going, darling; we still need to keep moving and find somewhere safer. Then we can rest."

The farmer approached, his hand outstretched, "Thank you so much. Now you really have saved our lives. We'll never be able to repay you."

I shook his hand. "It's fine. Remember, I was protecting my family as well. If you could help us out with the things Shawn asked for, then we'll get going. We really want to stick to our plan and keep moving."

"Of course. Just drive up to my barn and I'll get you what you need. If you could just give me a minute, I'll start getting everyone organised."

He was a natural leader and in no time at all, had issued instructions for everyone to start gathering the equipment they would need to start building their defences.

Once he was satisfied that everyone knew what they were doing, he climbed into Shawn's car and we all drove the short distance to his outbuildings. Once there, he introduced us to his wife and quickly updated her on what had happened. Then he instructed her to get us some food from the pantry.

She must have been made of stern stuff, because she took it all in her stride, remarked that they'd better get the cows in before they were eaten, and announced her intention of putting a bag of food together for us. She invited Becky and the kids to accompany her to the kitchen.

We followed him into the barn. He was clearly an organised man, because it was spotless and the shelves and racks were neatly stacked with a whole array of items.

He quickly found a six metre by six metre tarpaulin and an empty twenty five litre water container, which he started filling from a tap on the wall.

"Now what weapons were you thinking of?" he said, gesturing towards his tools.

"I could make a spear from a length of wood but an axe would be useful," replied Shawn thoughtfully.

"A hand or a felling axe?"

"Both if you have them. I normally have a hand axe with my kit but stupidly, I've left it at home."

"Here you go," he said and handed Shawn one of each.

I'd been rummaging through some of the shelves and had found a heavy looking machete in a sheath. Feeling that I was pushing my luck, I asked for it anyway. He'd been more than generous as it was. He handed it to me without hesitation, assuring me that he had plenty of tools.

Shawn asked if he had any diesel, as he'd made his escape from the garage earlier without filling up. Once again, the farmer was happy to oblige. A truly unselfish and generous man.

As we carried our gifts back to the car, he pointed to his diesel tank and told Shawn to back up to it, joking that he'd better not get stopped by the police, as it was red diesel and they didn't take kindly to ordinary motorists using it. He even asked if we wanted to take a few jerry cans of fuel with us, an offer we would have been stupid to refuse. So of course we didn't.

By now Becky had emerged from the farmhouse carrying a large bag of food. I was anxious to get going again.

I'll admit that the thought of staying and helping these people had occurred to me, but I'd quickly decided that moving on was the right thing to do. We needed to find somewhere really remote for a while.

I made sure that everyone was safely in the car and then walked up to our farmer friend, shook his hand and thanked him for the last time. As our small convoy drove away, I realised that I'd never even thought to ask his name. Everything had happened so fast. I glanced in my rear-view mirror and sincerely hoped that we'd given them enough time to prepare themselves for the horror they would be facing before too long.

The route we'd quickly traced out proved to be the correct one. For the first thirty minutes we didn't see another soul. Every house in every hamlet or small village we passed through was deathly quiet. Whether everyone was dead or just quiet we didn't know.

It was possible that everyone was following the government's advice and staying indoors. I wasn't sure. But I did notice that there weren't many cars parked on driveways or outside houses.

One explanation might have been that, on hearing the news, most people had assumed that it was a local event and decided that the best course of action would be to go somewhere else. Or more worryingly, perhaps the virus had spread so effectively that the locals were now all zombies.

Had we been the lucky ones, and by pure chance, somehow escaped becoming infected?

I thought it through. The UK had a population of over sixty million.

By the morning of day two of the apocalypse, the number of people actually infected or who had already transformed into a zombie would be huge, but surely this still only accounted for a small percentage of the population as a whole? The few people who had followed the government's advice and remained isolated from everyone should have survived day one without being infected. The rest, unfortunately, would have run in all directions. Human beings are social animals and we automatically seek safety in numbers.

The majority would probably have escaped the initial outbreaks, but then fallen victim to the unprecedented way in which the virus spread.

~

It was not yet midday on day two, but by the time Tom and his family were setting out for the moors, more than half the population of the UK had succumbed to the virus, as it raged uncontrollably like a wildfire sweeping through a tinder dry forest.

~

We kept the radio tuned into the emergency broadcast but it was still repeating the original message. We turned down the volume until it was just background noise, but so that we would hear if the message changed. Becky also kept checking her phone but it continually showed "No signal".

"I can see another car coming," I said quietly, and relayed the information to Shawn via the radio. A silver Ford Mondeo estate car was approaching down the narrow country lane.

It was an old model and had two surfboards attached to its roof rack. I slowed down and the other vehicle did the same, until we were about fifty metres apart from each other.

We all sat there for a while. I was unsure about what to do next. We could always just squeeze past each other and continue on our journeys, but somehow making contact seemed the right thing to do. If nothing else, we could use the opportunity to exchange information.

I flashed my lights, hoping that the other driver would interpret this as a friendly gesture. They returned the flash.

"Oh well, here goes nothing," I muttered to myself. I put on my mask and stepped out of the car. Shawn joined me.

Two young lads stepped out of the Mondeo and started to walk towards us. When they were about twenty metres away I held up my hand. "That's far enough please, we don't know if you're infected."

"We don't think we are," one of them replied. "We've listened to what the broadcasts and internet feeds that are still working have said. But the internet went down about an hour or so ago. We haven't been near anyone, but we've seen enough to know that it's true, and that there are zombies walking about. It's getting fucking freaky out here!"

"Where have you come from?" asked Shawn.

"Scotland," said the other one. "We've just driven down to try out the surfing. We were driving through the night and didn't know what was happening until a few hours ago when we got bored with listening to my music and turned the radio on and heard the emergency broadcast."

At that point, they explained, they'd suddenly realised that the roads were unnaturally quiet. They'd checked Facebook and YouTube and seen enough crazy videos to make them turn around and head back for home.

They'd been prevented from doing so by a massive crash about ten miles back up the road, which appeared to have just happened. They'd been about to get out and help when they'd seen one of them feeding on someone right in the middle of the road.

"We panicked," the lad said. "We just turned off the main road and ran into a field, smashing through the fence. Luckily it's been really dry lately, so we managed to get across a few fields until we found another road. We haven't got a map and my phone's map stopped working. so we got lost. We've learned enough to realise that we need to stay away from people, so we've been trying to find somewhere safe.

The problem is, we keep coming across the zombies. They're freaking everywhere! The last village we went through, we had to run two of them over to escape. They surrounded the car as soon as we stopped at a junction"'

I looked back at their car. It did look as if it had been through a lot; it was coated in mud and the front bumper and bonnet had big dents in them. Most of the body panels were damaged and one of the wing mirrors was hanging off.

I thought for a second. These guys had been driving through the night, so they couldn't have been in contact with anyone. It was pretty much the same as it had been with Shawn. We'd been in contact with other people but so far had shown no signs of being infected. We were, I concluded, incredibly lucky.

According to their story, there had been infected people in the villages they had passed through and they had seen more of them further up on the main road at the scene of the crash.

This confirmed the scale of the outbreak; it just had to be everywhere. The radio report had spoken of it being a global event and that had to be true. It couldn't just be confined to this remote part of Cornwall.

Logic dictated that the infection rate in the towns and cities must be almost 100% if we were coming across them in reasonably remote places.

I took a deep breath and spoke, "What do you want to do, lads? Neither of you has a Scottish accent, so why were you driving from there? My name's Tom by the way, and this is Shawn."

They both looked relieved. "Hi," said one. "I'm Andy and this is Chet. We've been in Scotland for the past week or so checking out the surfing and sleeping in the car. Chet got a call from a mate of his, telling him how great it was round here, so last night we decided to pack up and head down."

"If you don't mind me saying, you don't look like typical surfers," I said, eyeing them both.

"Why?" Chet replied indignantly, "Because I'm Indian and he's overweight?"

I had to laugh. I shook my head. "No! Well there is that, BUT I was about to say you both look too sensible to be sleeping in cars and chasing the surf."

Andy chipped in, "I'll have you know, weight's an advantage when it comes to surfing! But to be fair, Tom, you're right. We were both getting fed up with sleeping in the car; it just sounded fun when we came up with the idea. Chet's mate is staying at his parents' holiday home and he's got spare bedrooms, so we jumped at the chance of a soft mattress."

Shawn looked at them. "Where were you going to go when you decided to turn round?"

"We'd decided to head back to the student house we share in Birmingham. We haven't got any family around. Chet's still live in India and my parents have buggered off on a round the world cruise." He paused then looked upset, saying quietly, "I hope they're ok."

"Zombies!" shouted Becky suddenly, and we all started and looked round. A zombie was pushing its way through the hedge close to the car. Looking through the gap, we could see more behind it. Chet and Andy watched open-mouthed as I ran up to it, gripped it tightly by the hair with one hand and drove my knife through the side of its head with the other. I examined it as it lay sprawled on the ground. It was female and was dressed like a serious rambler with walking boots and proper hiking trousers. There was even a rucksack on its back.

"Look Shawn," I pointed out, "She hasn't been bitten as far as I can tell. She must have been infected another way. This virus is out of control! You haven't been near anyone who's infected and neither, apparently, have these guys (I pointed to Andy and Chet). We must have been incredibly lucky not to pick it up back at that campsite we were on. We need to set off for the moors now so that we can get ourselves organised."

I turned to Andy and Chet and for the first time, noticed their faces. "Don't worry," I said. "I couldn't have done that two hours ago either. It gets easier." Coming to a quick decision I continued, "Look, do you want to come with us? We're from Birmingham as well, so we may try to get back there …"

Shawn shouting, "Tom!" made me turn. The other zombies must have been closer than I'd realised as more of them were now forcing their way through the hedge. It was a hawthorn and the vicious thorns were ripping through their flesh and their clothing.

Oblivious to this, their horribly blank faces set in a kind of mute obstinacy, they pushed even harder in their desperation to reach us. I swallowed hard and Shawn and I stepped forward with our knives held ready.

The first few were relatively easy to kill, because they were caught up in the thorns but more kept on coming.

It dawned on me with horror that there were far too many of them and I started to panic.

Frantically, I killed one and pushed it away and then just managed to get another before it took a bite out of my outstretched arm. I scrambled backwards and glanced at Shawn. He was in an equally precarious situation and was desperately trying to kill as many as he could while avoiding being grabbed. I heard the engine of my car start and thought, *"Thank God, at least Becky will be safe,"* as I stabbed the nearest one through the eye.

I turned my head to see Shawn topple over, clutching a zombie by the neck to keep it from biting him. Suddenly the Volvo shot forward, and with a sickening thud, smashed into the zombies directly in front of me, knocking them over. It reversed, and with tyres squealing, rammed into the ones behind, clearing a space around Shawn.

That fantastic woman had kept her cool and thinking quickly, had realised that the only way to save us was to use the car as a weapon.

I thrust my knife into another one, and realising that Shawn was still in serious trouble, ran over and dragged the zombie off him. I dispatched it with a quick stab to the brain.

I pulled Shawn to his feet and handed him his knife which he'd dropped, then screamed, "Come on. Let's get out of here!"

"No!" panted Shawn, pulling away from me. "Zombie Rule Number 1. Kill every one of the bastards that you can. If you leave one, it could be the one that gets you later on."

He flung himself forward and began to work his way methodically through the ones Becky had knocked to the ground. Some of them had mangled limbs and were twitching like fish out of water, and others were attempting to stand up, their uncoordinated efforts making them look like drunks.

If it hadn't been for the fact that they were zombies, it might have been comical to watch. After watching him kill the first few, I stepped forward to help.

I felt something yank me from behind and realised that a zombie had grabbed hold of my jacket. I felt its rasping breath against my neck as it tried to bite me. I spun wildly and shoved it away, then stumbled backwards clumsily, falling hard against the side of the car. Dazed, I lost my balance completely and fell over.

The zombie lurched forward with obscene eagerness, a greedy look on its face. It was heavy and it took all my strength to push it away and stop it from biting me.

Its breath stank and I gagged. Its eyes were just six inches from mine, the normal blank gaze replaced by a look of burning hatred and hunger. The seconds passed and I felt myself weakening. I was struggling to push it away and its teeth were getting closer. A snarl escaped it and I tried to scream but no sound came out. I had nothing left. I was going to die.

Thwack! The zombie's head jerked to one side as something hit it. Smack! It jerked again. The third hit made a horrible squelching sound and I watched as the side of the zombie's skull caved in.

It went limp and fell off me, then lay to one side, either dead or stunned. I wasn't sure which, so I grabbed my knife and stabbed it for good measure.

I looked up. Standing over me, with his blood-flecked cricket bat gripped firmly in his hands, was my son.

What can I say? My ten-year-old son had just killed to protect me.

I stood up, my legs still wobbly, gave him a bear hug and said, "Thank you, son, I'm proud of you."

Becky stepped out of the car and I could see that, because she loved him, she was going to tell him off for putting himself in danger. Instinctively, I knew it would be the wrong thing to do. If he hesitated the next time it could get him or someone else killed.

I turned to her. "Don't say it," I whispered urgently. "We should be proud of him. If he hadn't realised the danger I was in and stepped forward, I'd be dead now or about to turn into a zombie. In my eyes, he's a man now."

Becky protested, "But he could have ..."

"No," I said firmly. "He wasn't and that's the point. Come on. We need to get moving."

By now Shawn had finished off the rest of them. They must have been a walking party who'd been infected at the same time, as most of them were still carrying their rucksacks. Shawn used his knife to carefully cut the straps and remove them from their previous owners.

I noticed that Chet and Andy were still just standing there, off to one side. *"They're going to have to get with the programme soon or there'll be no point in them coming with us,"* I thought, irritated. Yes, it had all happened very quickly, but it had been my young son who'd had to step forward when it counted, and they'd just stood there gawping like tourists.

Shawn must have been thinking the same because he said abruptly, "Come on, you two. Lend a hand. Let's check through these bags in case there's anything we need."

They seemed to pull themselves together and ran forward, eager to help.

The bags contained a few useful items, including a small cooking stove, a quantity of hot drink sachets and some snack bars and food. They'd also been carrying various items of waterproof clothing and some survival blankets.

All very handy, so we condensed everything down into two bags and threw them into Shawn's car.

We explained again where we were going and the boys immediately agreed to follow us. And why not? In the middle of a zombie apocalypse, I'd want to stick with proven zombie killers, and we'd just given them an excellent demonstration of our group's abilities.

I asked them to find a weapon so that they could help us next time. After searching their car, they came up with a tyre iron and a screwdriver. I gave them a quick demonstration of the best way to kill a zombie and gave them a rough plan of the route we were intending to follow.

They turned their car around on the narrow lane by backing it into the hedge, and then followed us as soon as we'd passed them.

That morning we'd been four and now we were eight.

Chapter thirteen

The journey from St Agnes to Bodmin took less than an hour when road conditions were normal.

Road conditions were not normal.

We were intentionally driving the "long way round", taking care to avoid all the main roads. Becky had Shawn's O.S. Map on her lap and was doing a fantastic job of guiding us through the countryside, avoiding as many villages and towns as she could. Whenever a turn was coming up, she would tell me first and then notify Shawn via the radio. She'd also adjusted the mirror so that she could use it and I could just concentrate on the road ahead.

I was becoming increasingly worried about the children. After saving my life, Stanley had come down from the adrenaline high caused by his actions, and was now looking exhausted. Daisy and Eddie still seemed completely strung out by all the stress of the situation.

Given everything that had happened, our interaction with the children had been confined to ordering them about and keeping them physically safe. We'd had no time to give any consideration to their emotional welfare.

I was having a hard enough time trying to grasp the situation myself, so getting everyone to safety was my primary concern, and it would have to stay that way for the time being.

We made our way tentatively through the Cornish countryside and by good fortune, didn't encounter another soul for the next three hours.

Eventually, as I was beginning to need the toilet quite badly, I asked the kids if they needed to go. It quickly became obvious that they were also desperate, but had been too afraid to ask me to stop and had been holding it in.

I stopped the car on a stretch of road overlooking the town of Bodmin. We were surrounded by open fields and therefore had clear views all around us.

By unspoken agreement, Shawn, Chet and Andy positioned their cars bumper to bumper with mine to create a rough triangle around a "safe" area in the middle of the cars. Before I let Becky and the kids out of the car, Shawn and I did a quick sweep of the area, to make sure that there were no nasty surprises hiding anywhere.

Becky and I took the children to a suitable spot and we all thankfully emptied our bladders. Then we quickly ushered them back to the safe area.

When everyone had followed suit, we all stood for a while in silence, our eyes naturally drawn to the smoke shrouded town of Bodmin.

"I hope we don't have to go through there," said Chet, shivering.

I looked down at the town. There were obviously fires burning out of control in several places. I shook my head. "No chance. If it looks bad from up here it's got to be freakin' awful down there. Shawn, let's get the map out and see if there's a way around."

Becky retrieved Shawn's map and spread it out on the bonnet of his car. Before long we'd managed to plan and agree a route that avoided Bodmin completely, and took us through country lanes until we reached the Moor.

Shawn explained that he'd camped by a small lake there previously and that it would be remote enough to keep us safe at least for the night. Once he'd found it on the map, we agreed to trust his judgement and head for it. Before we carried on, he insisted that we all have something hot to drink, and took out a small metal stove from the back of his car.

He picked up a few small sticks from the ground and put them at the bottom of the stove. Then he lit them and placed a saucepan of water on top of the fire.

The little stove was amazing, and in no time at all the water was boiling. I got some mugs from our car, and using the coffee we'd hastily packed in our food bag, I made us mugs of sugary coffee. We gave the children a can of coke each and I handed round some chocolate bars for good measure.

We immediately felt the benefit of the drinks and the chocolate, the sugar and caffeine giving us all a much needed energy boost. Just a few sips made us all feel more alert, as the stimulants in the drinks did the job that Shawn had intended.

Thanking Shawn, we made another quick study of the map and set off. The first mile or so was just as uneventful, but I had the uneasy feeling that our luck was about to run out. Yet as we continued through the narrow country lanes there was still no sign of anyone.

The road we were on gradually became steeper, the banks on either side of us growing higher and higher as the road turned into a traditional Cornish sunken lane. The feeling of being hemmed in intensified. I leant forward in my seat and gripped the wheel tighter. I couldn't explain it. It might have been paranoia due to the stresses of the day, but I knew we had ridden our luck for hours now. Something was going to go wrong.

And it did.

As we rounded a steep bend, I was greeted by the sight of a minibus stuck halfway up the bank and completely blocking the road. A body, which I took to be the driver, was lying motionless, half in and half out of the bus, having been thrown through the windscreen.

The radio crackled. 'Can you see anything?' asked Shawn, the tension in his voice transmitting clearly over the radio waves.

I could see that the side door of the bus was open but I couldn't see anyone else.

"No," replied Becky, "just the driver, who looks dead."

I sat in silence for a minute, considering our options.

Should we reverse back up the lane and find another route?

Should we get out and try to move the bus?

Could I push it out of the way with my car?

I was reluctant to leave the safety of the car if I didn't have to, so I decided against getting out. I could see past the van and noted that there was a cutting in the high banks to gain access to a field on a bend just ahead. If I could push the van off the bank, the chances were that the minibus would roll backwards guided by the narrow lane and high banks. Hopefully then it would just roll into the field and clear the way for us. This seemed like a better option than reversing and I couldn't make the roadblock any worse than it was, so I decided to give it a go.

I put the car in drive and slowly drove forward until my bumper was nudging the minibus. Then very carefully I increased the power to try to push it out of the way. The minibus moved slightly and then stopped again. I applied more power but it wouldn't budge. The Volvo's engine roared ineffectually and all four wheels spun. No luck. I backed off the power for fear of breaking anything and reversed back a few metres to see what the problem was.

It was obvious when you looked. The front wheels of the minibus were at the wrong angle. All I was doing was pushing it against a large tree, and I wasn't going to win that battle.

I was going to have to get out and turn the steering wheel on the minibus myself if it was going to go anywhere. I looked at the bus and my heart sank. A head appeared and something stood up in the minibus.

We now knew why the bus had crashed. We watched a zombie, its face covered in blood, trudge to the front of the bus carrying a severed arm in its hands. If it had been capable of curiosity I would have said it wanted to know what had interrupted its meal. You couldn't hear it with the car windows closed and the engine running, but it didn't take much effort to imagine the groans and snarls it was making as it gnashed its teeth through the window at us.

I was about to pick up the radio to tell Shawn that we would have to reverse and find another route, when the blaring of Chet and Andy's car horn made us all look round.

A large group of zombies was making its way down the lane.

We were in the middle of nowhere. Where the hell had they come from?

Andy revved his car and reversed as fast as he could in an attempt to force a way through them. There were too many of them and he stalled the car against the solid barrier of zombie flesh that was jammed in between the steep banks. He pulled the car forward and tried again, but apart from leaving a few zombies with broken bodies, struggling and thrashing on the floor, he was unsuccessful.

Luckily the lane was so narrow that the zombies couldn't get past the boys' car that easily, and they formed a pile of writhing bodies as they fell over each other in their desperation to squeeze between the car and the steep bank in order to get to us.

We only had a matter of minutes. I had to get the minibus moving.

"Becky, climb over and drive," I said, undoing my seatbelt. "I need to deal with that bus."

I didn't give her a chance to respond, but jumped out of the car and pulled my knife from its sheath. I waved at Shawn to indicate that he should stay where he was, and ran over to the bus. I could see the zombie inside watching me, and as I approached the open side door it immediately made a move for me. As it lunged, I didn't pause to think. I ran my knife through the side of its head, shoved it to one side and climbed aboard the bus. I couldn't tell how many dead were on the bus because the bodies were badly mutilated, but the one thing I was certain of was that none of them would be able to do me any harm.

The driver had lost most of his lower torso and legs so his seat was a mess of blood, scraps of flesh, bones and clothing. I looked up the road. Three zombies had managed to push past Chet and Andy's car and were banging on Shawn's car window. Thankfully they hadn't reached the Volvo yet but I knew I had no time to lose. Grimacing in disgust, I pushed what was left of the driver out of the way and sat on the sticky residue that remained.

I put my foot on the clutch, turned the key and prayed under my breath.

This had to work or we'd be in serious shit.

The starter motor whirred and turned the engine, but agonisingly it didn't catch.

I tried again, but the battery was dying, and the starter motor gave the characteristic but gut wrenching last few slow turns before it died.

"SHIT!" I screamed.

I was going to have to do this the hard way. Grabbing the steering wheel, I put all my strength into turning the tyres in the right direction.

It was hard going, as they were stuck in the soft banks of the country lane, but with the sweat rolling down my face, I realised in panic that more zombies were approaching.

I have read in the past that in times of extreme peril, the human body is capable of amazing things; acts of superhuman strength, for instance, when forced to harness it. This was one of those occasions. I am sure there is no way that under normal circumstances I would have had a hope in hell of freeing those wheels from that bank. But I managed it.

The handbrake wasn't on and I still had my foot on the clutch, so as soon as the wheels were released and were pointing in the right direction, the bus started to roll backwards down the hill. I didn't have time to look back at the others as the bus gained momentum and gathered speed. The large side mirrors gave me just about enough of a view to enable me to roughly steer the bus towards the gap in the bank. I bounced the minibus off both banks, but the bus had enough momentum to keep going.

I risked a quick glance through the windscreen and was relieved to see all three cars following closely, although Shawn's car had a zombie clinging stubbornly to its bonnet. The bend was approaching rapidly, so I tried to aim the bus towards the gap.

"Oh, bollocks!" I groaned, as more zombies appeared in the mirrors. They were staggering up the hill. As I approached the bend I could see further down the lane. More of them were on their way.

I made a split-second decision not to aim for the field but to use the minibus, with its weight and momentum, as a battering ram. Then I gritted my teeth and steered the bus down the hill.

I couldn't tell the others what I was planning to do; I just had to hope that they would work it out.

Bang! The first zombie was hit by the back of the bus, now travelling at a respectable twenty miles an hour. I felt a bump as it went under the wheels. I fervently hoped that Becky would realise what was happening, and increase the gap between us so that she'd avoid the bodies. More smacks and bumps followed as the heavy bus steamrolled over everything in its path.

I tried the brakes, but with no power to the engine they were soft and hardly slowed it at all. I lifted my foot off the clutch to try to use the gearbox to slow my descent, but the van was in first gear so the wheels locked and almost made me lose control.

If I'd been thinking clearly, the obvious solution would have been to attempt to jump start the van, but I was too busy trying to control it and steer into the few remaining zombies I could see.

The road ahead looked clear now, so putting all my weight on the brakes and feathering the clutch, I tried to bring the bus under control. It slowed gradually as the hill bottomed out, and as the road widened, I steered the bus into a wall in an attempt to stop it. Eventually, after much screeching of metal and the destruction of a perfectly good wall, the bus came to a halt, leaning at an angle with its rear axle sitting on top of the damaged wall.

I jumped out of the bus and saw more zombies pouring out of the door of a hotel across the road and heading straight towards us. Most were dressed in suits and posh frocks. The two wedding cars outside, bedecked in ribbons, told the story of someone's dream day that hadn't quite worked out the way they'd intended.

No wonder there were so many zombies around in what we'd hoped would be a quiet back road.

Shawn got out of his car, killed the zombie that was still clinging obstinately to the front of his car, removed it from his bonnet and walked over to me. "You're a bloody nutter, mate!" he said, beaming.

I would have loved to relax for a while, but the next wave of wedding zombies was only fifty metres away and getting closer.

Nodding at them, I replied, "Let's discuss my stupidity later. We need to keep moving. We should only be a few miles away from the edge of the moors now."

Chet and Andy had rolled down the windows of their car, which was looking considerably more beaten up and wouldn't have looked out of place on the starting line of a stock car race. Both side mirrors were now hanging off, it was covered in dents and the rear window had a hole in it, presumably from a zombie's head going through it.

After a quick exchange to check that they were ok, I ran back to the passenger side of the car and climbed in. We had no time to swap drivers and besides, Becky had already proved that she was up to the job when she'd saved all our lives earlier.

Chapter fourteen

We pulled away just as the first zombies reached us. As we drove past the bus I sent it a silent "thank you". The fact that it had been blocking the road could well have caused our deaths, but in the end, it had redeemed itself in its last wild ride down the hill. It rested forlornly atop the damaged wall, most likely never to move again.

Scanning ahead to make sure the road was clear, I leant over and gave Becky a quick hug and a kiss on the cheek, then turned to see how the kids were doing. Eddie was still sitting quietly, but both Stanley and Daisy were wide-eyed with excitement. They jabbered on about how I'd crashed the bus and Mommy had had to drive over the bodies in the road. I let them carry on. It was probably their way of coping with what was happening, trying to normalise what was, let's face it, a very untypical experience for them. Untypical for all of us, in fact.

I managed to get them to calm down by asking them to carry on keeping watch out of the windows for more zombies. Previously we'd occasionally played "I Spy" to entertain the children on long car journeys. Now we were playing "I Spy a Zombie!".

I noticed a junction up ahead and hurriedly picked the map up off the floor where it had ended up after Becky and I had swapped seats. I quickly found our location and gave Becky instructions. I could see the edge of the moors rising ahead and hoped that they would offer us the sanctuary we needed. Shawn had shown me a track on the map which, from memory, he thought would be suitable for cars and would lead to the lake we wanted to get to. I kept my finger on the spot on the map and carefully guided us to it.

I asked Becky to slow down when I thought we were getting close. Great! Ahead I could see the outline of a track leading across the moors and disappearing over a hill.

I warned Shawn via the radio to get ready to turn, and saw him put his indicators on to warn Chet and Andy behind him. It was a grass-covered track, and as Shawn had promised, it was just about suitable for cars. With some careful steering, you could get through the bumpier parts without too much trouble. With its high suspension and four-wheel drive the Volvo managed with no trouble at all. Becky slowed down to allow the other cars to keep up, as they were having to be much more careful to avoid damaging anything vital. The last thing we needed now was a breakdown.

Slowly but surely we climbed the hill. The views were impressive, and the higher we got, the wider the vista became. As we crested the hill the lake appeared in the distance, nestled in a small fold of the land. Looking around, there were no man-made features to be seen. The place was remote and isolated. Exactly what we needed.

The lake was in a small valley and looked idyllic. There were even a few trees, which had managed to grow together in a small copse, sheltered from the constant, howling winds the moors were known for.

Becky pulled the car off the track at its nearest point to the lake. The other two cars joined us soon afterwards. Instructing everyone to stay in the car, I climbed up on to the roof of the Volvo with my binoculars, and after carefully checking that the area was free of all traces of zombies and humans, I happily reported that it was safe to get out.

Chapter fifteen

Becky and I helped the children out of the car. They were obviously nervous but we kept assuring them that it was safe. I noticed that all the adults, unconsciously or otherwise, joined Becky and me to form a protective ring around the children, and was touched by their concern.

We stood there looking at each other in silence. Everyone had a weapon of some kind either in their hand, or attached or shoved through their belts.

Words couldn't begin to describe the day we'd experienced, but for the moment we were safe. Stanley and Daisy naturally gravitated towards Becky, who automatically put her arms around them. Eddie stood to one side, looking awkward and uncertain about what to do next.

I noticed this and said, "Come here, champ." As he walked over, I put my arm around him. "You're going to be ok now. Don't worry, we'll look after you."

Tears began to stream down his face and he wrapped his arms around me. "I want my mum," he wept. Knowing that he needed to grieve for the parents who had been so brutally slaughtered in front of him, I said nothing, but just held him tightly.

He was young and in time, hopefully, he would come to terms with what had happened. Like him, we were also going to have to accept that our friends and loved ones were probably dead or zombies by now.

But not today. Today he just needed to let it all out.

As I stood there holding him and listening to his raw grief, I found myself crying too, as the full impact of what had happened began to sink in. I looked around. Everyone seemed to be feeling the same.

Still hugging Eddie, I moved over to Becky and the kids and we all had a group hug, as we expelled the collective emotions of the day. Chet and Andy clung to each other for support and Shawn sat down, held his head in his hands, and from time to time, quietly wiped his eyes.

Ten minutes later I was feeling calm but incredibly tired, as the last of the adrenaline drained out of my system. Everyone was clearly feeling the strain. I extracted myself from our hug and gave Becky a gentle kiss. She kissed me back and then sat on the floor, still hugging the children, who all seemed better for having had a good cry.

I walked over to Andy, Chet and Shawn, who were all looking distinctly embarrassed.

"Well," I said, clearing my throat. "I think we all needed that!"

They all chuckled and nodded. The mood lifted.

I looked at Shawn. "You're the expert, what now?"

Shawn considered our surroundings for a few minutes. "Well, last time I was here I just hung my hammock in the trees, but if memory serves me, there should be an old drystone-walled sheep pen in the copse as well.

The walls aren't that high, but they should give us some protection. But before that we need to plan escape routes, in case we're attacked again."

We all looked round nervously.

Shawn laughed, "Don't panic. If I see one, I'll be shouting louder than that. Tom, could you get my map out of your car please?"

He spread it out and the four of us leant over to study it. He looked at it for a minute or two, then pointed with a finger. "This is where we are. As you can see, the track we've been using carries on over the next hill.

There's a farmhouse over there and I imagine it connects to that. The farmhouse should have a drive connecting it to the nearest road."

He pointed to another "B" road that cut across the moors.

As one, we all looked up towards the track, which wound its way up and over the next rise.

"If we spot any zombies, and there are too many for us to deal with, I would suggest that we just drive in the opposite direction. If for some reason we can't use the cars, then we'll make our way on foot in the opposite direction, and just carry what we can."

Looking serious, he said, "I know it sounds obvious, but if we all agree about it now, it'll save having to decide about it if the shit hits the fan. Tom, you'll need to make sure that Becky and the kids know all this as well."

I nodded.

"That reminds me," Shawn continued. "Once we've set up camp we'll need to organise a grab bag for everyone, just in case we have to get out fast. Nothing too complicated; it just needs to contain food for a few days, if we have it, plus a few essential bits of kit."

"Like what?" Chet asked.

"I don't know what we've got yet, mate. Once we've sorted through everything, I'll let you know. But right now our priorities are shelter and food. If one of us stays on lookout duty, the rest of us can start setting up camp."

Andy volunteered to be the first lookout, so I handed him my binoculars. He climbed up a small rock formation and sat and scanned the surrounding moorland.

Leaving Becky still consoling the children, the three of us walked the short distance to the small copse of trees.

The sheep pen was there, and was just as Shawn had described it. Its walls, although in a poor state of repair, would still serve as an effective barrier against zombies (provided that they weren't too good at climbing!).

At Shawn's suggestion, we decided to use the tarpaulin the farmer had given us to make a roofed shelter which would be large enough for all of us to use.

As we walked back to the cars for the equipment we needed, I told Chet about the encounter we'd had with the farmer and the villagers, and how generous he'd been in giving us supplies, equipment and extra weapons. While Shawn was getting the stuff he needed out of his car, I went to sit by Becky.

All three children were calmer and were cuddled up close to Becky as they watched our progress. Becky and I exchanged a look. Given the circumstances, they were as happy as could be expected.

I mustered up all the cheerfulness I could manage. "Hey kids, we're going to be staying here for tonight at least. I'm going to need your help to set up camp if you feel up to it. Do you want to come with me?"

What great kids. I wanted to keep them busy for obvious reasons and they didn't disappoint me. We soon had them busy fetching this and holding that, and in no time at all the tarpaulin was in position. Shawn skilfully set it up so that it created a covered area easily big enough to accommodate us all.

He'd cut a branch from a tree and used that to raise the front up, creating a half-pyramid shape. We all listened attentively as he explained that he had set it up so that the front faced away from the prevailing wind. If the forecast from the previous day was correct, then we should be in for at least another week of dry weather, so the shelter would be more than enough for our needs.

If we ended up staying longer than that, he would easily be able to build a more robust structure, using the materials around us.

He hummed as he worked, clearing loose rocks and stones from under the tarpaulin.

"Are you actually enjoying yourself?" I asked.

"Of course not, but you wouldn't believe the number of times I've thought about this. This is a perfect opportunity for a prepper: bushcraft and a zombie survival plan all rolled into one!

Last time I camped here I clocked it as a good bug-out location, suitable for lots of different events, including the fabled zombie one. I've planned for this so many times in my head, it almost comes as second nature. Look around and I'll explain."

He led us around like an eager tour guide. "We have a lookout as the first line of defence, so we can concentrate on setting up camp first and not have to worry about perimeter security. Once I've moved these rocks and stones out of the way, I'll go to that fence you can see over there, and remove as much wire as I can from along its length. Then I'll form another perimeter around us as our second line of defence, using the wire fencing." We listened attentively, impressed by the amount of thought he'd put into it.

"While I'm doing that," he continued, "I want the rest of you to concentrate on rebuilding the wall as best you can and also to come up with a way to block the entrance up. When all that's done," he explained, "we'll have a three-layer warning/defence system. All the zombies we've seen have been slow moving, much like the stereotypical zombie we're used to seeing on TV. We'll learn more about them as time goes on, but for now our best policy would be to avoid them if we can.

Yes, we need to kill as many as we can as often as we can, so we can deal with small groups of them like we did earlier, but if they start moving around in packs, the layers of defence will alert us and hopefully they'll slow them down enough to allow us to escape."

For a moment we were all silent, thinking through what he'd said. "Does that make sense?" he asked anxiously, clearly concerned that we hadn't understood him.

Chet spoke for all of us when he said, "It sounds like perfect common sense, now you've said it. But would we have known what to do if you weren't here? We might have worked it out eventually, but at what cost? We might still all end up dead, but with the head start you've given us, I feel like we stand a much better chance."

We all nodded in agreement.

Shawn looked pleased. "Right then," he said, "let's get finished and then get some food down us."

Andy shouted down from his rocky perch, "Can we swap now? I feel like a bit of a spare part up here, while you're all doing the hard work. I feel like I should be doing my bit."

I looked up at him. Andy and Chet had come a long way since our first meeting, when they'd just stood to one side, watching us fight off the zombie hikers. They were rapidly going up in my estimation.

They were likeable young men and although they'd had no other option, they'd shown a lot of courage in using their car as a battering ram when we'd been trapped by the crashed minibus. "I tell you what mate," I shouted back, "you're a lot younger than me, I'll swap with you."

I turned to the others. "Anybody else wanna go first?"

Both Shawn and Chet said they were happy for me to go. Then I looked at Becky. She grinned, shook her head and said, "Do you really want the most short-sighted person here on lookout duty? I don't think so. You go on up. The kids and I will be fine down here."

I smiled at her and climbed up the rocks to where Andy was sitting. He pointed out some landmarks, and also where the sheep and ponies were.

"First ponies I saw, I almost shit myself! They looked like a crowd of zombies until I got my hands to stop shaking and took a proper look!"

As he climbed down I got comfortable and checked out the area, both with and without the binoculars. The view from the elevated position of the rocks was great; you could see for miles in each direction. It was a shame my binoculars weren't more powerful, but they were all we had, so they would have to do.

As I sat there, I had the first real chance to dwell on what had happened over the course of the day, and think about the future. We had to assume that this plague was everywhere. We were in one of the remotest and least populated areas of England, and we'd still encountered them, and the last news broadcasts had suggested outbreaks all over the country.

How we'd managed to escape the virus was beyond me, but somehow, either by luck or fate, we'd avoided it so far. Meeting Shawn had been an enormous stroke of luck and we'd never have got to such a remote part of Bodmin Moor without him. Whatever happened in the future, I would always owe him a debt of gratitude for that.

Throughout the day, aside from the few cars we'd seen in the morning and the villagers who'd isolated themselves, we hadn't come across another living person; only zombies. Granted, we'd been avoiding populated areas, but even so, this was worrying.

That got me thinking about the numbers we might be facing. The population of the UK was about sixty five million, so if, at a conservative estimate, around five percent of the population were not infected (and therefore not a zombie), that worked out roughly as sixty two million zombies versus three million people like us. Not good odds at all.

~

As it turned out, at the end of day two, Tom's rough estimate wasn't that far out. Millions of people were still surviving around the country. The more fortunate ones had securely barricaded themselves in, or were in a remote location and had sufficient supplies to last at least for a time.

Others were less fortunate and were unsuccessful in escaping the roving packs of zombies. Hundreds of thousands more were trapped in their homes or offices, with no hope of escape or rescue, as the zombies laid claim to most of the country. Anyone stuck on their own, or hiding out in small groups, too frightened to venture out, faced dying of thirst or starvation over the coming days and weeks.

All government personnel – the police, the armed forces and medical services – had virtually ceased to exist. The police and medics went first as they were initially on the front line. Military personnel were hit next. The rapid spread of the virus led to widespread outbreaks on most bases, immediately rendering them ineffective.

The few unaffected regiments that were deployed by the government, soon succumbed either to the virus or to zombie attacks.

It was nobody's fault. Without time to prepare, the soldiers were deployed with only the vaguest orders to maintain public order and protect the general population.

Not understanding what was going on, most were attacked and overwhelmed by the advancing zombie hordes. When the survivors eventually worked out what was happening and began to use their weapons to save their own lives, it wasn't enough to make any difference. They were carrying only a basic load of ammunition, and had no access to new supplies.

Assault rifles with bayonets fixed were converted into spears and clubs, as small groups of surviving soldiers used their training to work together and fight their way to safety. Not many of them made it.

The Royal Navy fared better, as it had numerous ships and submarines out at sea, and therefore many were able to avoid the virus completely. As the top-level command structure collapsed, it was down to the individual skills of the commanders to ensure that their crews survived.

Sitting on his rock in the middle of Bodmin Moor, Tom was unaware of any of this. All he cared about was keeping his family safe and well, so his primary concern was figuring out the best way to do that.

~

Staying where we were would probably be ok for a day or two, but we were in an exposed position. If any zombies managed to find us, even with defensive measures in place, these would only serve to slow them down.

They wouldn't be enough to protect us in the long term. The weather on the moors was also known for being extreme at times, one of the reasons why the military had based so many training operations there. Come wintertime, it would not be a good place to be based with your wife and three young children.

We needed supplies and suitable shelter. We couldn't possibly take on and destroy millions of zombies. The only option was to separate ourselves from them and try to survive as best we could.

But how?

I carried on thinking.

Chapter sixteen

Under Shawn's supervision, the camp was really taking shape. He'd surrounded the place with a two-strand wire fence, using the many trees that surrounded the old sheep pen as posts. He told me later that the idea had come from watching the "Walking Dead" TV series, where they seemed to do that a lot at overnight camps when they were hiding in woods.

We'd rebuilt the wall to the best of our abilities and Becky and the children had been busy cutting bracken and heather to use as mattresses. We'd even managed to use Chet and Andy's surfboards to create an effective barrier to block the entrance.

Shawn called me down from my lookout post, as he wanted us all to carry out an inventory of what equipment and supplies we had. I wasn't too concerned, because even at ground level you could still see for quite a distance all around.

Before we'd even begun, I'd spotted a potential problem with what we were about to do, so I decided to raise the issue first. "I think we need to decide before we proceed: are we treating ourselves as a group and sharing everything equally, regardless of who owned it in the first place?"

Shawn shrugged. "I'm happy to do so, but we'll all need to agree on this now. It'll save any arguments in the future."

Andy spoke up, "To be fair, Chet and I hardly have anything to contribute apart from a few Pot Noodles and some rice. We were mainly living off fish and chips and beer when we were in Scotland. We've got a camping stove but we hardly used it. I'm up for sharing, but you have to understand that we don't have a lot to offer."

"You're right, Tom," said Shawn, "I don't have much packaged food to offer either, but let's not worry about food too much; we're surrounded by it.

I love foraging, and without even trying, I could get enough food just from this immediate area to give us all a good meal. I was thinking more in terms of the equipment we have. It would be better to spread it equally among us, otherwise the loss of one car or one bag could be disastrous."

"Fair point, Shawn," I replied, "we can't argue with that logic."

In the end, very little had to be distributed. We divided the food we had into equal piles and put a similar sized bag into each car.

It was the weapons we had the biggest discussion about. Shawn had one extra knife in his bag in addition to the ones he'd given to Becky and me, and apart from the machete, two axes and my probably useless "knife on a stick", all we had was Stanley's cricket bat, some tyre irons and some screwdrivers.

Chet took the hand axe and that left Andy with a choice between the machete, a knife and a long-handled axe. He chose the machete because with its sheath he could attach it to his belt.

We decided that the axe should be carried as an extra weapon by whoever was on guard duty. Shawn put the extra knife on his belt as a spare.

We knew the knives were effective for killing zombies, but weren't keen on the fact that you had to get so close to do it. A weapon with a longer range would be safer, but for the time being we would have to manage with what we had. When Daisy walked up to me and whispered that she was hungry, we realised how late it was getting and that none of us had eaten anything substantial since breakfast. Chet and Andy hadn't even had that, as they'd driven through the night straight into the zombie apocalypse.

As it was the middle of summer, there were still a few hours of daylight left, so while Becky and I set about heating up pans of food on the two gas cookers, Shawn foraged some flowers and leaves to make a tasty and colourful looking salad.

With the help of the children, he gathered up a stack of dry deadfall branches and quickly got a reasonably smoke-free fire going. It wasn't cold, but the reassuring warmth from the flames and the crackle of the dry tinder made the camp feel a little cosier. As we all tucked into the meat and pasta we'd prepared, we complimented Shawn on how tasty his salad was. Even the kids had tried and enjoyed it.

It consisted, he explained, of dandelions, daisies and navelwort, all extremely nutritious and plentiful at this time of year. Impressed, we all insisted that he should start sharing his knowledge. He tried to make a joke of it, pointing out that this would be a good idea, as he might be dead tomorrow. Nobody laughed. We were only too aware of the precariousness of our situation.

After we'd eaten, one of the others went to keep a lookout and Becky and I got the children, who by now were all extremely drowsy, settled down at the back of the shelter under some blankets.

It wasn't long before they were all fast asleep.

As darkness began to fall, the rest of us sat around the dying embers of the fire. We were all aware that it was best not to keep a blazing fire going, as this might advertise our presence to others, alive or dead.

Realising that it was pointless trying to keep a lookout in the increasing gloom, we agreed that while the rest of us sat around the circle of stones containing the remains of the fire, one of us would remain standing and stay alert. That, we reasoned, ought to suffice.

We'd gathered together all the torches in our possession and shared them out. I had a very powerful LED torch which I kept in the car at all times and between us we had a variety of head torches and smaller handheld ones.

For the moment, there were enough for us all to have one each, plus a few spares.

Shawn went to his car and returned with several bags. "This is one of the goodies I told you about earlier. It's a crossbow. I always keep it broken down and hidden in various places around the car."

"Why?" asked Chet, intrigued.

"Well, although it's not illegal to own one, it's easier to keep it disassembled than have to explain why you've got it. Under the current law it's illegal to hunt with them in the UK, but most preppers, myself included, favour keeping a few of them around, because let's face it, when the shit hits the fan who cares?

Now I'd say a whole ton of shit has hit the fan, so it's probably time to get it out. They're good for large and small game and obviously for defending yourself. Remember 'The Walking Dead'? It was the only thing Daryl ever used."

We watched as he removed various pieces from the bags and deftly assembled it. "They're easy to maintain," he explained, "and if you run out of bolts, it's not impossible to make your own."

He passed it round so that we could all handle it. It was a deadly looking piece of equipment, painted with a camouflage pattern, and with a small telescopic sight attached to the top of it. He explained that it would easily be powerful enough to kill something at a distance of fifty metres or even more, but then the obvious problem would be accuracy.

At a distance of twenty to thirty metres he thought he should be able to get in some consistent headshots.

I handed it back to him. "That's a great weapon. I think we should see if we can all get one. I feel a bit happier now that we've got something that'll kill them from a distance. But I did a lot of thinking while I was on lookout duty, and I think we all need to discuss and agree on the best course of action to take."

No one commented, so I continued, "We don't know how far this thing has spread, but from what we've seen today, I think we'll have to assume that most people are now dead or zombies.

There will also be other people who've been lucky enough to survive. Perhaps they're having the same conversation as we are now." I looked at Shawn, "Please feel free to interrupt if you disagree."

He nodded and said, "Yes, but carry on. It'll be interesting to hear someone else's perspective on what's happened, and what we can do. In the groups I belonged to no one ever agreed on anything, apart from the fact that it was going to happen at some point. It's vitally important we do now. To survive this situation, we've all got to be on the same page."

No one else said anything, so I added, "We can't stay here long term; we're too exposed. If a pack of them appeared over that hill we'd have no choice but to move on, and if that happened in the middle of the night it could easily go wrong. What we need is somewhere that can give us proper shelter. We also desperately need supplies and, if we can find them, some decent weapons."

I looked around. Everyone was nodding. "I imagine that the one thing that will be in plentiful supply will be food. Every supermarket and shop in the land will have full shelves and hardly anyone will be needing it.

We should be able to take whatever we need, when we need it, but in the long term it would be sensible to source a large supply that will keep us going for a long time. That would avoid the risk involved in constantly going out and gathering it."

"We're going to have to find some better weapons. Your crossbow is great, Shawn; a real asset. I have a few shotguns at home, but I can't for one moment imagine that it's worth driving all the way to Birmingham to collect a few shotguns, when there must be plenty of them around here.

Most farmers have shotguns, and possibly rifles, and what about the police or the army? If we know where to look, they must be around here somewhere. We could just get the Yellow Pages out and find the nearest barracks or gun shop."

I paused, then asked the question: "So where do we go? Well, we also need somewhere that will offer constant protection so that we're not living in fear of zombies appearing all the time. We need solid walls. While I was up on the rock, I went through all the places I could think of. But most of the obvious places: prisons, hospitals and army bases, are probably full of zombies already. We need to go somewhere where people don't live, so that we can clear it of zombies when we get there."

The others leaned forward expectantly.

"We need to find an intact castle" I said seriously.

Everyone just looked at me.

Chapter seventeen

Everyone continued to stare at me, then Shawn smiled and started quietly clapping.

"Well done mate," he said, grinning. "I don't think anyone could have put it any better. You've just described the best way to survive a zombie apocalypse. It is, when you think about it, just common sense after all. But as my old man always said, 'There's nothing common about sense!' My mates and I used to talk about this over many a pint in a pub, but the one major flaw in your plan is the 'intact castle' bit. Every castle I've ever visited has either been a ruin, or it's got so many holes in its walls, it would be impossible to defend. There's nowhere suitable for what you want!"

Becky interrupted him smiling, "Shawn, do you or any of your friends have children?"

"No, why?"

"Where do you live?"

"Bristol, why?"

"Have you ever heard of Warwick Castle?"

I smiled as I realised she knew exactly what I was on about.

Shawn frowned. "Not really, is it in English Heritage or The National Trust? I think I've visited most of their places on my travels, so I may have been there, but it doesn't spring to mind straightaway."

Chet interrupted now. "I know it! When my parents came over to visit last year we went there. Shawn, it's completely habitable. It's got proper walls, gates, moats, everything. It even impressed my parents, who are a bit snobbish and say that Indian culture outdoes everything else.

If it's still like I remember it, it would be a great place to use. It's run as a big tourist attraction and is owned by some big group."

Becky nodded eagerly. "That's right, and it's in Warwick; hence the name. Tom and I have taken the kids there many times. It really is in remarkable condition, given that I believe it was originally built by William the Conqueror. If we could get the gates closed, it would be pretty much impregnable to zombies. The accommodation area's huge and in good condition. Great idea Tom, darling!"

She turned to Shawn, who was looking a little crestfallen. "Shawn, don't worry, if you haven't got kids or you're a tourist, you probably won't have visited the place."

We all sat in silence for a while, lost in our own thoughts.

Shawn spoke first, "I think, unless we can think of somewhere closer, it's a great plan." He pulled his phone out of his pocket and checked it, then sighed because it still wasn't working.

He shoved it back into his pocket. "This would be a great time for a bit of googling. I bet within half an hour we'd have all the information we needed to make the right decisions. Can we think of anywhere similar to Warwick Castle? It's a great idea, but there might be somewhere even better ... I tell you what, let's get the map out. It might remind us of somewhere we've been."

He spread his O.S. map out and Andy got his UK road map from his car and we all spent the next twenty minutes studying them by the light of our torches to see if any ideas "jumped off the pages". We managed to identify and mark on the map most of the castles and other places, such as old manor houses. We also picked out prisons and any buildings that might be surrounded by a secure fence or wall.

The same problems were evident with all of them; if they'd been inhabited by people, then they were likely to be full of the undead, or the security provided by the fences or walls wouldn't be adequate.

The best alternative we could come up with was St Michael's Mount, an island accessible by foot at low tide, just off Cornwall's southern coast near to Penzance, which we'd visited a few years before on our last holiday in the area.

Despite its beauty and its advantage of being reasonably close to our current location, we ended up discounting it. It seemed unlikely that we would be able to secure the island from any potential zombie invasions at low tide, and after a quick check, we concluded that none of us was very competent at sea fishing and using boats. If we had to rely on the sea for our food we weren't sure how successful that would be.

I stood up to take my turn as the lookout, leaving them to discuss the merits and drawbacks of each of the places identified on the map. Warwick Castle was still looking like the best candidate, but in a way, I hoped that we'd be able to find somewhere closer. We were a good few hundred miles from Warwick, and the prospect of driving that distance through a zombie-infested England wasn't very appealing.

The conversation finally died out just as the embers in the fire lost their last traces of heat. The faces lit by the single small camping lantern we'd been using were showing signs of strain and exhaustion.

We were trying to keep our usage of lights to a minimum, and I'd walked about fifty metres away from the camp to check that the glow from the little lantern was barely visible before we'd decided that it was ok to use it.

Even though sleep was going to be hard to come by, we all knew that we had to rest.

After a brief discussion, we worked out a guard duty rota. I volunteered to take the first shift. Andy and Chet had had no sleep the night before, because they'd driven through the night, and Shawn had admitted to only managing a few hours due to sleeping in his car.

There were a few awkward moments when they realised that the mattress of bracken and heather meant that the sleeping area would be quite cosy when they all lay down, particularly as Becky would be lying next to them.

Becky made a few light-hearted jokes about no hugging and spooning, as she snuggled down next to the sleeping children.

After ensuring that everyone had their torches and weapons close to hand, I turned the lantern off and plunged the camp into darkness to begin the first guard shift. As my eyes adjusted, I marvelled at the amount of light given out by the moon and a myriad of stars, which covered the sky like a twinkling blanket.

It illuminated the scene in front of me, but the light also cast shadows. And when you're on guard duty in the middle of the night, on the lookout for bloodthirsty zombies, every shadow of every bush, moving and rustling in the wind, looks like a flesh-eating monster. I had no trouble staying alert.

Not feeling tired at all, I waited for three hours before waking Shawn up for his turn. He woke up immediately and I handed him my large torch and crawled into the shelter next to Becky.

I tried to sleep, but after an hour of struggling to lie still so as not to disturb her, it became clear that the one thing that would evade me that night was sleep. My mind was still running at a hundred miles an hour. Carefully, I scrambled out of the shelter and went to join Shawn.

I made us both a cup of coffee and we stood watch together, chatting quietly and gradually getting to know each other better. In what seemed like no time at all, the eastern sky began to lighten as a precursor of the approaching dawn.

There was a beautiful sunrise over the moors, and I felt privileged to have been able to witness it. The fact that I might meet a horrible death at any time probably made me appreciate nature's splendour all the more. One by one Becky, Chet and then Andy woke up and joined us. They all tried to admonish us for not having woken them, but Shawn and I were having none of it.

Keeping our voices as low as possible, so as not to wake the children, we planned out the day. I wanted to check out the farmhouse that was just out of sight over the hill. It was the nearest place that might offer us some solid shelter and I felt that we should at least see if it could provide us with more security than we had where we were.

The plan was unanimously agreed on. I wanted to set off straight away, but Shawn insisted that we deconstruct the camp we'd made and take it with us. He explained that he'd thought about this scenario a lot and it was always best practice to take everything you had with you at all times if possible. If you were unable to return for whatever reason, or the camp was overrun by zombies or another group of survivors (both potentially dangerous scenarios), then at least you'd still have most of your gear.

Once again, unable to fault his logic, we agreed and while Becky was gently waking the children, we began to take down and roll up the fencing wire we'd scavenged the day before.

Unsurprisingly Eddie quickly became distraught on waking, as the memories came flooding back. He was a brave boy though, and after a few minutes of comfort from Becky, he'd recovered enough to eat the breakfast we gave him.

We used most of the fresh milk for our cereal and for the kids to drink, and there was just enough left over to give us each a last cup of fresh milky coffee.

A shout from Shawn, who was on lookout duty, got us all scrambling to our feet. He was staring through the binoculars at the distant hillside.

"What's the matter?" I asked.

"Hang on, I thought I saw something. Wait, yes, two people heading this way. They seem to be rushing... oh shit! Zombies!"

Chapter eighteen

Shawn handed me the binoculars. It took me a while, but I managed to make out two people trying to run through the purple heather. They were so far away it was impossible to make out their gender, but the shambling gait of the figures chasing them was unmistakeable. Straining my eyes, I managed to count five zombies in total.

"So what do we do, guys?" I asked, passing the binoculars to Becky.

"Well," said Chet slowly, "You helped us, so I suppose it would be wrong not to help anyone else. There can't be that many people left alive, so I guess it's important that we all stick together. I'm no hero, but the human race needs all the help it can get at the moment if we're all going to come through this."

Andy butted in, "Blinking hell, mate, just because you're in the debating society there's no need to get all theatrical on us. But yes, I agree, we should try to help them."

Everyone nodded in agreement.

Unfortunately, the terrain was too rough to even contemplate using a car to reach them. Even the Volvo, with its high ground-clearance and four wheel drive, wouldn't make it fifty metres off the track. We were going to have use Shanks's pony; in other words, walk.

I made a quick decision. "Look, we're all going to have to go. If we leave the kids here, we'll need at least two people to protect them and, well, don't take this the wrong way, but only Shawn and I actually have any experience of killing those things, so I'd prefer it if one of us stayed with my family. But given that I can see at least five zombies over there, it's probably best if we're all on hand to deal with them."

"Dad," called Stanley. I turned to find him standing behind me holding his cricket bat. Eddie was beside him gripping my home-made zombie spear in both hands. "We can help as well. Eddie and I will protect Mom and Daisy."

Looking into the distance at the two objects of our discussion, it was soon clear that they weren't managing to increase their lead on the zombies. If anything, the zombies were rapidly gaining ground. They'd be in serious need of some help soon.

I took a deep breath. "Come on then, let's all go. Stanley and Eddie, if you could guard our backs and look after Mommy and Daisy that would be a great help."

It was the best I could come up with at short notice; the lesser of two evils. I would die before I let anything happen to my family and I was afraid that if they stayed behind, they'd end up in even greater danger if more zombies appeared.

Staying together seemed the best idea, and Stanley had already killed a zombie. Hefting the weapons we'd laid claim to the day before, we got ready to go. Shawn cocked his crossbow and fitted a vicious looking barbed bolt into the groove. He put a bag over his shoulder containing more bolts. I grabbed the large axe and made sure my knife was still in its sheath.

Chet and Andy stood around looking nervous, clutching their respective machete and axe.

Just as we were about to set out, Shawn unclipped the spare knife from his belt and walked over to Daisy. Smiling gently at her, he knelt down and clipped it to her belt. Then he looked at Becky. "It's better that she has it so she'll at least have the chance to defend herself."

I could see that Becky was about to protest, when Daisy spoke up, "Mommy it's ok, I know what I've got to do. Everyone else has got something to fight with; it's not fair if I haven't."

I intervened hastily, "Becky, it's fine. I'll give her a good talk later about knife safety. Thanks Shawn." Then I looked at Daisy. "Do NOT get that knife out unless you're in danger, do you understand? Leave this to the grown-ups. Now, come on everyone, the zombies are almost on top of those people. What the hell is making them so slow? They should easily be able to outpace them!"

As we set out across the moor, I found myself reflecting on the bizarreness of our situation, and I almost laughed out loud. Less than twenty four hours ago I'd been packing the car for a day at the beach with my family. Now we were all striding across a moor, armed to the teeth, hoping to save two people we'd never met before from zombies. In a few minutes I'd be driving my knife through the head of someone who'd once been a normal person.

As we got closer to them, we could see that the people in trouble were both women and were clinging to each other for support. One seemed to be having trouble walking and the other was helping. They hadn't noticed us, so I shouted but they clearly couldn't hear me. Shawn finally managed to get their attention by blowing loudly on a whistle, and they responded by waving and changing direction towards us. Unfortunately, this shortened the distance between them and the zombies who, distracted by Shawn's whistle, began to make their way over to us instead.

"This is not good." I thought. *"They're going to get caught by them unless we do something."*

"Becky, keep the kids with you. If anything happens to us, run back to the cars and drive away." Throwing caution to the wind, the four of us started sprinting across the moor. It was going to be close. We were all running together, holding our weapons ready.

"We need to distract them," I gasped between breaths. Our shouting and hollering had confused the zombies, who seemed to be struggling to work out the best food sources to aim for: the quiet ones closest to them or the noisier ones further away. Two of them suddenly turned back towards the women and three of them continued on towards us. One of the women fell over, dragging the other one down with her, their shrieks of terror prompting me to run even faster.

"Chet, with me. Shawn and Andy, get the others!" I panted, as I headed towards the women.

As I ran past the outstretched arms of the nearest zombie, I swung my axe wildly at it. The blow, poorly aimed, failed to hit anything vital, but did succeed in knocking it off balance. As I ran on, the blood pounding in my ears, I could hear Chet breathing heavily beside me. The women were trying to get back up, but their panic was making them clumsy. I was ten metres from them when the two zombies reached them and fell upon them.

I dropped my axe, knowing that if I swung it now it could easily injure one of the women as she lay writhing on the ground, and instead pulled my knife from its sheath. The woman's screams pierced the air. There was no time to give Chet instructions; he knew what he had to do.

The long hair of the nearest zombie proved a bonus. It was so intent on feeding on the woman, it had forgotten all about me. I grabbed a fistful, pulled its head back and stabbed it as hard as I could.

It instantly went limp, as it died for a second time. Still clutching its hair, I pulled it off the hysterical woman.

The other zombie was also stone dead. Chet was standing over it, staring at his hand axe, which was sticking out of its head as if it was stuck in a log. I immediately turned to check on Shawn and Andy, and watched Shawn neatly dispatch the last three zombies from a distance of about ten metres, with crossbow bolts to their brains.

Beyond them stood Becky and the kids. They immediately became my first priority and I walked over to them, saying, "Shawn, see to the ladies please. I'll go and get Becky."

I grabbed Becky and gave her a hug, then turned to Stanley, Daisy and Eddie. "Thanks for protecting Mom for me." Eddie showed no discomfort at my referring to Becky as his mom. In a sense, I suppose we'd already unofficially adopted him, so when we had time we would need to think carefully about how to deal with that. "Come on," I said to them. "Let's go and meet the new arrivals."

As we approached the others, I suddenly realised that something wasn't right.

The three men were standing around the women, who were both still on the ground holding on to each other. They were both crying.

Andy came to meet us, looking worried. "One of them's been bitten."

"Shit!" I said, "When?"

"Just as you got there, when they first attacked them."

I immediately felt guilty. We'd wasted precious minutes and seconds prior to going to help them. If we'd gone to them as soon as we'd spotted them, she might have been ok.

Becky, who knew the way my mind worked, said firmly, "Don't even go there, Tom. Do not even begin to blame yourself. You did your best."

"I know, love. Look, can you take the kids over there somewhere? You know what we're going to have to do."

I think the children already understood what was going to happen, but the urge to protect our kids from the outside world for as long as I possibly could was still overpowering. They all looked up at me and then over to the two women and then let Becky usher them away. I heard her saying, "Everyone else is going to be busy, so it's up to us to keep a good lookout."

As I got closer I winced at the sight of the bite wound on the woman's arm. A huge chunk of her bicep had been ripped away and blood was pouring from the wound. I certainly didn't want to get near the wound, as no one knew yet whether contact with the blood would transmit the infection. Up until now we'd got some on us when we'd been killing them, but as they didn't actually bleed that much, it wasn't a lot. This woman was bleeding profusely from an open wound caused by a zombie bite.

We knew they needed our help though, so I knelt next to her, taking care that the wound was on the side away from me. Both women were in their late twenties and dressed in jeans, trainers and t-shirts. I touched the uninjured one on the shoulder tentatively. She hadn't noticed me arrive and jumped violently at the contact. Her face was muddy and tear streaked, her eyes puffy from crying.

"Thank you," she said, trying to smile. "We've been trying to get away from them since last night, but they kept following. Please, you have to help Julie; have you got any bandages?"

I paused, not knowing how to break the bad news.

Shawn crouched down beside me. "I'm sorry," he said, as gently as he could, "There's just no easy way to say this. If she's been bitten then she's probably only got about ten minutes before she becomes one herself. We've seen it before."

She stared at us indignantly. "No! Look at her! She's ok, it's just a bite. She can't be one of them. What are they anyway?"

Unable to restrain himself, Andy said, "Where have you been for the last twenty four hours? They're fucking zombies and they wanted to eat you!"

The look I gave Andy made him stop. He walked away holding up his hands in apology.

Shawn tried again. "Look, I'm really sorry, but from what we've witnessed, if your friend's been bitten, then it's likely she's going to turn and there's nothing we can do to stop it. The only thing we can do is wait. I'd suggest you say your goodbyes now." As he said it, he clumsily put his hand on her back in a vague effort to offer support.

For the next few minutes both women hugged, cried and denied that anything was wrong. Gradually the bitten woman fell silent and then slumped unconscious. We all sat poised, ready to react. Her friend, who was still hugging her, was clearly completely unprepared for what was about to happen.

I had to get her out of the way. I knelt close to her and put my arms on her shoulders. "Please. Just move out of the way for a minute. Let me check her. I know first aid so I'll put her in the recovery position. It'll help her."

She looked at me and nodded, wiping her eyes. My lie had worked and she stood up and stepped back a few paces.

It was only just in time. The woman's eyes opened, and she went into violent spasms as the virus took hold of her body.

With a cry, her friend stepped forward to help her but Shawn had anticipated this and quickly grabbed her and held her back.

Within thirty seconds the bitten woman had completed her transformation and was trying to stand.

I turned to her companion and said, "I'm sorry. I'm going to have to do this to protect us all."

I turned, grabbed the woman's hair and killed the newest addition to the zombie population.

Wearily, I looked at her friend, who was white with shock. "Shawn, when she's ready, bring her over to the cars. I'm going back to my wife and children."

Picking up the axe, I walked over to Becky and we all made our way back to the cars. While Daisy kept a lookout from the rock, I got everyone busy refilling the cars with everything we'd unpacked the day before. Ten minutes later Shawn, Chet and Andy appeared, accompanying the quietly sobbing woman. Now I'd had the chance to look at her properly, I could see that she was in her late twenties to early thirties. She had a slim athletic figure and long brown hair and was a very attractive woman.

Stopping what we were doing, Becky and I walked over to them. "I'm very sorry I had to do that to your friend," I began, "there was nothing else we could do." She looked at me, crying afresh, and sobbed, "She was my sister!"

I was stunned into silence for a moment.

Before I could say anything else Becky stepped forward and enveloped her in a hug, saying, "I'm so sorry," over and over.

This brought on a fresh bout of tears and the men stood around awkwardly, waiting for the emotional roller coaster the woman was on to slow down.

After a few minutes I indicated for Shawn, Chet and Andy to finish off packing the cars. While they were busy with that, I kept an eye on the children who by now had all climbed on to the rock to help keep a lookout. I smiled as I heard Stanley organising the others and telling them which area to scan.

A little while later, once Becky had managed to calm the woman down, she led her over to me. "Tom, this is Louise. I've explained to her what just happened and why her sister died."

"Hi Tom," said Louise. "I understand you had to do what you did. I know I'll never get over losing her, but I also know I have to be strong. Becky says I can stay with you until I reach my family."

I smiled, "Of course you can. Now we really need to get moving. Our car's pretty full so if you wouldn't mind travelling with Shawn, we're trying to get to a farm we know is just over the hill. Hopefully it'll be a bit safer for us there than out here in the open, so the sooner we get there the better."

Nodding, she walked over to Shawn's car. After a quick check to make sure we'd left nothing behind, we started the cars and with me in the lead, continued slowly along the track.

Now we were nine.

Chapter nineteen

I crested the hill, stopped the car and waited for the others to arrive. After a thorough check that the coast was clear (this had become second nature to all of us), we stepped out and looked across the moor towards the farmhouse. It was a solid building, surrounded by barns and store sheds, and nestled peacefully in a shallow valley. I looked at it carefully through my binoculars before passing them to Shawn. "It looks clear to me, what do you reckon?"

"Looks quiet," he replied. "The front door's wide open, so there could have been some trouble, but on the bright side, I think the place has an alternative power supply. I can see a wind turbine and there are solar panels on the roof of the barn. It makes sense really; they're so remote they must be vulnerable to power failures when the weather's bad." He turned to me looking positively cheerful, "I say we go and check it out."

I nodded. "Right everyone, let's stay close together. When we get there, Chet and Andy, you come with me to make sure the main house is safe, while Shawn stands guard outside with his crossbow. Then we'll go through the outbuildings, just to make sure they're clear as well. We'll work out the rest when we get there."

Soon afterwards we were driving through the open gate of the farmhouse. It all looked very quiet and apart from the fact that the front door was swinging slightly in the breeze, everything seemed completely normal. I squeezed Becky's hand, smiled reassuringly at the children, and stepped out of the car.

Shawn had his crossbow raised and was scanning the area constantly.

He instructed Louise to get out of his car and into mine. With my knife in my hand, I motioned for Shawn and Andy to follow me. Remembering that zombies tended to be attracted by noise, I banged loudly on the front door, pushed it open slightly and shouted, "Anyone at home?"

In response I heard the now familiar groan of a zombie from somewhere in the house, followed by someone calling out for help. The shouting appeared to be coming from beneath our feet, presumably from the cellar.

The zombie appeared in the entrance to the hall, dressed in a ripped and bloody pair of pyjamas. As it made its way towards us, I stepped back from the narrow doorway to give Andy and Chet room to stand beside me. One of its feet was sticking out at an unnatural angle, giving it an even more awkward gait than normal.

"Got one coming out," I shouted to warn Shawn.

"Ok, it's still clear out here. Be careful," he replied.

As I stepped forward and felled the zombie with a thrust of my knife, I found myself chuckling. He'd said it in the same way that someone tells you to be careful if it's slippy outside.

I looked at Chet and Andy and came to a decision. It was about time they took the lead. "Right," I said firmly, "One of you can go first. Let's make sure there are no more of them." To their credit, they actually argued over who should lead the way. Andy won, having promised that he would let Chet go first the next time.

Whoever was in the cellar was still shouting and hammering up against the floor. It sounded as if more than one person was down there, but it was difficult to be sure because the voices were muffled. All the rooms downstairs were clear so we climbed up to the next storey. The first bedroom we entered solved the mystery of the pyjama-wearing zombie.

A blood-spattered bed held the gruesome remains of a woman. Presumably the zombie had turned during the night and fed on his wife while she was sleeping. It was a sickening sight and not one of us was sufficiently inured to the horror of it.

We'd all seen similar scenes in movies, but this didn't in any way prepare you for the sweet smell of decaying flesh and the sight of flies buzzing over ruptured intestines. I could feel my stomach beginning to churn.

I shut the door, took a deep breath and said, "If we're going to be staying here we need to do something about that."

The house was large and had a lot of doors, so each one had to be opened very carefully in case it was hiding a nasty surprise. When we finally came back downstairs I tried a door in the kitchen and discovered that it was locked. As I tugged at the door handle I heard someone inside shout, "He's back! Get out of my way. We need to get away from the door." Clearly I'd found the entrance to the cellar.

"Hello!" I called. "We've er … we've killed the man in the pyjamas. Is there anybody else in the house we should know about?"

There was a pause while the person inside digested what I'd said. "No!" they said finally.

"I don't think so. That man fell down the stairs and tried to attack us yesterday. We've been down here ever since. He's been pounding on the door non-stop." The voice, which was clearly male, sounded very frightened.

I tried to sound as friendly as possible. "It's ok to come out now. We've checked all the rooms and the house is clear."

"Who are you?" said the voice distrustfully.

Andy once again displayed his undiplomatic side, shouting, "We're the ones who've fucking saved you! Who gives a fuck who we are? You're the idiots hiding in a cellar. We're not going to hurt you. Just man up and get out here!"

Lost for words after that blunt but accurate appraisal of the situation, I gave Andy a severe look. Then I told him to stay with Chet and carry on trying to persuade them to come out. I walked out of the house to check on Shawn.

To my surprise they were all out of the car and standing close together. Shawn was standing on his car bonnet with his crossbow at the ready. He greeted me cheerfully. "Hi, Tom. Don't worry, it's safe out here. The amount of noise you lot have been making would wake the dead, not just zombies. While we've been waiting I've carried out a sweep of the outbuildings. They're all clear."

Momentarily annoyed that he'd put himself in a potentially dangerous situation which could have had a direct impact on my family, I opened my mouth to say something, but then thought better of it. He wasn't daft and had obviously assessed the situation as being low risk.

While we were waiting for Chet and Andy to coax the people out of the cellar, I took the opportunity to look round. The whole farm was surrounded by a solid drystone wall, about four feet high.

There were two five-bar metal gates at either end of the yard to give access onto the moors.

The walls would help to shelter the whole place from the weather, and I suppose in days gone by, the farmers would have brought all the sheep inside the enclosure when the weather really took a turn for the worse.

All I cared about was the fact that it looked secure. I went to look at the barns.

They contained all the things you'd expect: a newish looking tractor and a quad bike, plus other pieces of equipment in various states of disrepair. I was tempted to investigate further but I heard Becky's voice calling me back.

The people in the cellar had finally emerged and were standing quietly next to Chet and Andy. They were a couple in their mid-fifties, dressed in walking gear, and were looking decidedly dishevelled. The man was fiddling nervously with his mobile phone.

The children were looking slightly shocked and the others were all looking furious.

"What's up?"

Hands on his hips, Shawn spoke first. "Mr Knight here wants to report us for murdering the poor man who tried to eat him. We've been trying to explain to him what's been happening in the world, but he assures us that that's just not possible.

I've even shown him the remains of the man's wife, but he insists that an animal must have done that, because God wouldn't allow something like this to happen."

The gentleman in question walked up to me, held his phone up to my face and took my picture.

"What the hell do you think you're doing, you idiot?" I snapped, irritated.

"I've taken photos of all of you!" he squeaked in a nasal voice that I found instantly annoying. "I insist that you take us to the nearest police station where I shall report you all. Shame on you for exposing your children to your cruel, godless ways. Maud! Come and stand next to me and get away from these people."

He stood with his arms folded, a superior look on his face, as his wife meekly joined him.

I was lost for words. I truly didn't know what to say to the man.

For the first time Louise spoke up. "Are you completely stupid or something? Everyone's turning into zombies! These people saved my life less than an hour ago. My sister and I were hounded across the moors all night after our car was surrounded by them. My sister was bitten and she turned and then they had to kill her. It wasn't murder! They were saving my life just as they did yours when they killed that man in the house who'd turned."

"Maud, come with me," said the man, beginning to inch away from us. "We can't stay here any longer. We're in danger. She's just told us they've murdered someone else. I have their pictures; they won't escape."

We stared at him in disbelief. The man was clearly deranged or something. All attempts to reason with him proved fruitless.

Once again, Andy summed up the situation. "Let them go. I can't put up with his whining voice for another minute. We've tried to explain what's happening, but they just don't get it. Chet said earlier that we should help everyone to ensure the survival of the human race. I'm sorry but he's wrong, we can only help people who want to help themselves."

He turned and addressed them again. "What were you doing in the farmhouse anyway?"

We watched as the man puffed out his chest indignantly and went slightly pink in the face. "I was going to make a complaint to the farmer. He'd left some barbed wire sticking out of a post and I caught my jacket on it and tore it!" He held his jacket out and showed us a small tear in the lining.

Before any of us could respond, Becky suddenly lost it. "For God's sake, just go!" she said, through clenched teeth.

"If you're too stupid to realise when someone's trying to help you, then just leave! Go and find the police. And good luck with that! I guarantee we're not going anywhere for at least the next day or so."

She advanced on them and the man backed away, grabbing his wife by the arm and shouting, "Look Maud, they're attacking us now! Let's get out of here before they kill us too."

We watched in astonishment as they hurried out of the gate and along the track that led to the road.

I shook my head and turned to everyone. "Right, let's get this place secure and then we can sort ourselves out. Louise, if you don't feel up to it that's fine."

"No, no," she said quickly. "I want to help. It won't do me any good brooding."

I nodded in approval. "Great, well done. Becky and the kids and I will check the perimeter while the rest of you look for something we can use to strengthen the gates. They look like the weakest points to me."

Chet and Andy set off to check one building, and Shawn and Louise walked over to the other, while we walked around examining the walls. The place was as good as I'd hoped, and unless the zombies turned out to be good climbers, then providing we could secure the gates I was reasonably confident that we would be safe for a while.

Chapter twenty

As predicted, the walls were solid enough, but the gates were definite weak points. They opened outwards but were only held closed by a single metal catch. The catches looked sturdy enough, but I doubted if they would be strong enough to hold back zombies en masse.

We still didn't know enough about what they were able to do. We'd only experimented on the woman in the Range Rover to see how they could be killed. Were they capable of climbing up and over obstructions? The ones we'd seen previously hadn't done that, but we'd watched them get back up after being knocked down so it was probable that they could climb stairs and therefore also negotiate their way over things.

Shawn was busy wedging lengths of timber against the gates to reinforce them. He was doing a good job, so I led Becky and the children into the house so that we could explore it.

I moved the farmer's body out of the way to save the children from having to step over it. I'd never had to move a dead body before and was shocked by how heavy it was; it took all my strength just to drag it off the path.

I'd warned Becky beforehand about the room containing the woman's body so we were able to avoid the children inadvertently opening the door and seeing her. I also wanted to keep the disgusting smell confined to the room if at all possible. The house already contained faint traces of it, but as the heat of the day began to build, it was only going to get worse. We needed to remove both corpses as a matter of urgency.

I tried a light switch and was pleasantly surprised to find that it worked. I also noticed that the cooker in the kitchen was a gas one.

The house was too remote to be connected to the mains, so I reasoned that they must have a propane tank somewhere. If the electricity and gas were still connected and working, we'd have hot water for washing and cleaning.

As we explored the house, the news got even better. Both the pantry and the freezer were well stocked with food, so we wouldn't have to worry about going hungry just yet, and apart from the bedroom containing the body, there were five more, so there would be enough beds for all of us. I'd discovered a gun safe bolted to a wall in the boot room of the house and was trying to find the hiding place for the keys so that I could open it. I'd also found quite a few boxes of shotgun cartridges and another small locked safe in one of the downstairs cupboards.

I was hopeful that it might be where he kept his rifle bullets and that there would be a rifle in the gun safe (I was aware that the rules about storing bullets were far stricter than they were for cartridges). If I wasn't able to locate the key, we would have to find a way to break into them.

The only weapon we currently had at our disposal which could kill from a distance was Shawn's crossbow and that took time to reload. A shotgun or rifle would make a big difference to us.

Becky had found a leaflet advertising the farm as a bed and breakfast business that also offered evening meals. No wonder there was so much food around.

The children had spotted the TV in the lounge and had gathered in front of it like moths to a flame. They'd switched it on but hadn't been able to find a single broadcasting channel that wasn't displaying the emergency message.

Realising that we hadn't listened to the radio all day to check for updates, I went to the kitchen where I remembered seeing one and turned it on, tuning it in to the right frequency.

I caught the end of a message stating that the broadcast would be repeated, so Becky and I sat at the kitchen table and waited for it to begin again.

Our hearts sank. It was repeating the same message as the day before. Either there was nothing new to report or there was no one left to update the message.

The sound of a TV playing made us rush into the lounge so see what was happening.

The kids had found some DVDs and managed to put a movie on. Becky and I watched them from the doorway for a while. It was a Simpsons DVD and in no time at all my two were roaring with laughter at Bart and Homer's antics and even Eddie was managing to smile.

Becky put her arm around my waist and her head on my shoulder as we watched the children. Over the past two days they'd seen and experienced the most mind-numbingly terrifying things. Only yesterday, Eddie had watched his parents die and Stanley had saved my life by caving a zombie's skull in with repeated blows from his cricket bat. Now they were laughing at some mindless comedy on the TV.

We came crashing back to reality, as Chet came running into the house yelling, "Zombies!" The pleasure on the children's faces evaporated and was replaced again by terror. They looked at us. Becky hugged me even more tightly and then said, "Go! I'll get the kids upstairs."

I ran outside to find the others looking in the direction of the track that led to the nearest road. Shawn was squinting through a set of binoculars that I hadn't seen before. I looked at them as he handed them to me.

"They were in the tractor," he explained. "They're good ones. It's that prick, Knight, and his missis. They're on their way back and they've managed to bring a whole load of zombies back with them."

I looked through the binoculars. They were so powerful I felt as if I could have reached out and touched them. The Knights were staggering along, their faces white with exhaustion and terror. It proved the point that you could outrun zombies over a short distance, but their pursuers were relentless in their pursuit of food; a "tortoise and hare" scenario (and we all know how that ended!). The zombies were clearly able to keep going until exhaustion overtook you and you could go no further.

I don't know how long the zombies had been chasing them, but it was clear that the Knights were almost at the end of their endurance. They'd probably already been worn out by their ordeal in the cellar.

I tried to count the zombies and guessed that there were around forty of them. As I watched, I was shocked to see Knight grab hold of his wife and push her behind him. He was clearly intent on putting his wife between himself and the pursuing zombies.

"Fucking prick!" I exclaimed. I passed the binoculars to Andy and described what I'd seen to the others.

Without hesitation, Louise spoke up, "We should help her. I felt sorry for her when he was ranting on earlier. She looked really embarrassed and kept glaring at him behind his back. He's probably been bullying her for years and she hasn't had the confidence to stand up for herself."

"I agree we should help her," said Chet, "but what about him?"

"I'm not making that decision," I said. "But in the meantime, we've got forty zombies heading our way and we're in no way ready for them. We need to get that gun safe open and I haven't managed to find the keys yet."

"Tom, I've just thought," said Shawn, "There's a petrol-powered disc cutter in the shed over there. I know how to use them, so I should be able to cut into it. Look, two of you need to go and get the Knights. The rest of us need to stack everything we can up against those gates."

I nodded and looked up at Becky and the children, who were watching us through an upstairs window. We were going to need them so I waved for them to come and help. I clapped Chet on the back. "Come on mate, it's your turn to be the hero now."

Becky came out just as I was running to our car and I shouted to her, "Can you open the rear gate? I'll be back as soon as I can."

As she opened the gate, I quickly drove out and bumped along the track that led outside the walls, until I'd reached the main track that led to the gate closest to the Knights and the zombies. I'd made a snap decision to exit using the gate furthest from the zombies, figuring that it would give the others more time to reinforce the gate before they got there.

Looking ahead, I could see that Maud was falling far behind her husband, who wasn't paying her the slightest bit of attention. She'd virtually come to a standstill, and looked as if she'd more or less given up. The track here was in better condition than the one we'd used to get to the farm. I suspected the farmer had maintained it because it was their main access route. This worked in my favour because I was able to drive reasonably fast along it, only having to swerve to avoid the bigger potholes.

As we approached, Knight stood in the middle of the road and waved his arms frantically. "I really hope you're not planning to get him first!" said Chet grimly.

"No way!" I kept my speed up and drove straight for him. I knew the coward wouldn't have the nerve to stand there and I was proved right, as he dived out of the way just as I sped past him.

"Get ready, Chet," I said, gritting my teeth. "You need to get her in the car. Be careful, they're close behind her."

He gripped his hand axe tightly and the car skidded to a halt next to Maud. As he stepped out I watched as he swung his axe, cleaving the head of the nearest zombie, then pulled it out and smashed the next one in the side of the head, almost taking the top of it off in the process. That bought him the time to grab Maud and push her into the back of the car.

There was no time or space to turn the car around so I slammed the car into reverse, turned in my seat to face my new direction of travel and started heading back to the farm. Looking at Maud, I said, "Don't worry, we'll get your husband."

She looked at me, wild eyed, the tears drying on her cheeks and said, "Don't you dare get that bastard, he just told me to stay there and die so that he could live."

Chet turned to her. "And you did?"

"I decided I'd had enough. I might as well die. It would save me having to spend another minute with that man. He's made my life hell for thirty years."

I slowed down as we approached him. He was standing at the side of the track and as we got closer, he began to bang on the car, his face red with fury, demanding to be let in. Not knowing what to do, I drove past him and he began to run after us, thumping his fists on the bonnet and screaming furiously for us to stop.

"Stop the car," Maud said quietly.

I did as she asked. He made his way round to the driver's window and began hammering on it with his fists, demanding that I get out and let him drive. Chet had put his hand axe in the footwell. Maud leant forward and before he could stop her she'd grabbed it, opened her door and stepped out to face him.

Mr Knight turned on her immediately. "Maud, get out of my way!" I watched, stupefied, as she suddenly swung the axe and hit him on the side of his head. It was a glancing blow but seemed to invigorate her because she swung the axe again, with renewed force. The resulting slice took his ear clean off and the axe stuck in his shoulder. She pulled the axe out and he fell to the ground, his face pale and shocked, then tried to scramble away from her, all the time screaming and pleading for her to stop. She followed him, raining blow after blow down on him until he was lying motionless. Seeing that the zombies were almost level with us, she calmly walked back to the car, climbed in and handed Chet the bloody axe, which he took without a word. She made no comment, but sat there on the back seat, looking blank and slightly dazed.

Chet and I looked at each other and he raised one eyebrow. Not knowing what to do or say, I put the car into reverse and just as the zombies were within touching distance of the car, turned and sped back to the farmhouse.

I glanced in the rear-view mirror, just in time to see the zombies stop and cluster eagerly around the body, ripping at it frenziedly with their teeth.

"Well!" I thought, somewhat callously, *"That's probably the only unselfish thing he's done in his entire life. It's given us more time to get ready."*

Now we were ten.

Chapter twenty one

We arrived back at the yard to find that everyone had been busy. The gate had been firmly propped up with extra lengths of timber and Shane and Andy were dragging sheets of plywood towards it.

Chet helped Maud out of the car and we joined them. As we approached I just said, "Knight didn't make it." I exchanged glances with Chet and he nodded. It would be our secret.

Maud seemed to come to herself and said quietly, "Thank you."

"Right then, Shawn, what do you need us to do?" I asked, conscious that the zombies would be finished with the body before too long.

"Chet, you start propping up the rear gate, like we've done with this one. I'll come and help you in a minute. Tom, I managed to get those safes open. Why don't you go and check them out; I haven't had a chance yet."

The mood was tense, but everyone moved with a purpose. They were all, the children included, hurriedly carrying or dragging boards, steel roofing sheets or lengths of wood towards both gates and casting frequent anxious glances in the direction the hungry horde would be approaching from.

I ran into the house and made straight for the boot room, where the gun safe was. Its door was lying next to it with big holes cut into it. Shawn had obviously just cut the locks straight out. I was impressed as it must have taken some skill to be that accurate with the heavy piece of machinery he'd been using.

The contents of the safe made my day. There was an old looking side-by-side shotgun, a more modern over-and under-one, and a scoped rifle.

Quickly grabbing all three, I ran to the room where the cartridges had been stored in a cupboard. The contents had been strewn over the floor in Shawn's haste to open the smaller safe.

Once again, the door to the safe had been skilfully removed. Grabbing one of the boxes inside it, I saw that it contained .22 rim fire rifle ammunition.

I'd used rifles occasionally, so I knew that .22 rim fire was the standard rifle for small game and vermin. The farmer had probably used it for controlling the fox population on his land. I looked out of the window. The zombies were very close now, so I opted for just taking the shotguns because I was familiar with them. I didn't think I'd have time to work out how to load and operate the rifle. I snatched up two cartridge bags and stuffed them with as many cartridges as I could find, then I ran out of the door to join the others.

The zombies were almost upon us. All work had stopped and everyone had gathered together to watch them.

"What now?" I heard someone ask uncertainly.

"Who knows how to use a shotgun?" I asked.

"I'll stick with my crossbow," said Shawn firmly.

Both Chet and Andy shook their heads, but Louise spoke up, "I had a boyfriend who used to go shooting a lot and he encouraged me to have a go. I'm not the best but I have been game shooting with him."

"That'll do for me," I said, "which one do you want?"

She took the side-by-side, saying that it looked similar to the ones her boyfriend had given her to use. As she took it she broke the barrels open and inspected the gun. You can tell if someone is comfortable with a gun by the way they handle them, and she looked competent enough. I handed her one of the cartridge bags and she deftly inserted two cartridges and closed the gun.

I checked mine and loaded it.

The zombies were now just fifty metres away. Stanley spoke up. "Dad, I've counted them. I think there are fifty five."

"Well that's about fifty five more than I wanted to see," I remarked, wryly. "Shawn, what should we do?"

"I think we should wait and see what happens," said Shawn, thoughtfully. "They may just pass us by, although if they know we're in here, I doubt it. As long as they can't get over the walls, we'll be safe, but then again, the walls aren't high enough to hide us from view completely. If they stay at the walls, we'll have to kill them. I haven't figured out the best way yet, but now we've got a variety of weapons, I'm sure we'll find out by good old trial and error. The one thing we can't do is wait them out. We'll probably starve before they do, and we don't yet know if their presence here will somehow attract more. They may have a sort of zombie telepathy."

I just looked at him. "Telepathy?"

He shrugged and grinned. "Hey, everything was a theory until it was proved right or wrong."

The zombies were very close now. They'd followed the path of least resistance to us and that had led them directly to our weakest point: the gate.

I turned to Stanley, Daisy and Eddie, who were standing beside Becky and a still dazed looking Maud. Stanley was gripping his cricket bat and Eddie was holding his zombie spear, while Daisy stood with her hand on the handle of the knife Shawn had given her.

"Kids," I said, "I want you to stay here and protect Maud, but I also need you to be our eyes. We may be concentrating too much on one area and miss something going on somewhere else. The three of you need to keep a good lookout and tell us if we miss anything."

They all nodded, the determined expressions on their small faces showing courage far beyond their years.

The main gate started to rattle as the first zombies reached it and began to push up against it. More arrived. The gate began to groan alarmingly and some of the wooden supports fell down.

Shawn, Chet and Andy ran forward to try to reinforce it. It now had the combined weight of all the zombies pushing against it. I felt anxiety creeping up on me. We needed to get them away from the gate.

I picked up a spade, ran over to the wall just to the left of the gate and began shouting and banging it against the stone wall. Some of them turned, cocked their heads like dogs, and looked in my direction. I yelled at the top of my lungs and swung the spade even harder against the wall. It made a satisfying ringing sound.

Yes! They were beginning to move towards the noise I was making. I moved further away from the gate, drawing even more of them in my direction.

The rattling of the gate ceased, as they stopped pushing against it and made for me. Holding my position now that the gate was clear, I kept up the din until they were all gathered at the wall right in front of me, a mass of outstretched arms and contorted faces, reaching out, desperate to feed on me.

I risked a glance at the gate and was relieved to see the three men working furiously to strengthen it. My moment of inattention almost got me killed, as a zombie reached out and snatched the spade I was holding and yanked me towards him. My first reaction was to try to fight it but I was pulled dangerously close to the other outstretched arms. I screamed in fear and let go of the spade.

I staggered back, panting. The other side of the wall was now lined five deep with zombies.

The wall was nowhere near high enough and they were beginning to bend their torsos over the top of it. In desperation, I raised my shotgun, aimed it at the closest one and pulled the trigger. The gun kicked and the zombie's head transformed into a mess of blood, bone and brain. The hideous creature remained upright, held fast by the pressure of the ones behind it. I took aim at another and it was flung backwards by the force of the shot.

I noticed that the recoil was more than I was used to, so when I broke the gun to eject the cartridges and reload, I checked the new cartridges quickly before shoving them into the barrels. They were thirty-six gram fours which meant a good heavy load with a lot of stopping power. Ideal for pulverising zombie brains!

The problem was, now that one zombie was dead on the floor, the others had something to step on, which raised them up a bit more. And the more they leant over the wall, the more the weight of the others pushing from behind was virtually propelling them over it.

I heard Stanley, Daisy and Eddie shouting at the others to let them know.

As I shot and killed the two that were furthest over the wall, the others hurried over to join me. Shawn raised his bow and released a bolt that stuck in the head of another zombie.

Louise's first shot hit one of them in the shoulder. Oblivious to the fact that its arm was hanging in tatters, it resumed its efforts to get over the wall. Learning quickly, she readjusted her aim and killed it with a shot to the head.

The more bodies there were on the ground, the more difficult our situation became, as it made it easier for the others to climb on to the growing pile. We'd only managed to take out six of them and they were almost over the wall.

"Chet, Andy, go to the sides and try and get some," I shouted frantically, as I fired both barrels again. Louise's gun firing by my right ear felled two more. She hadn't been lying when she'd said she could shoot.

Chet and Andy ran forward, bravely trusting us not to hit them, and wielding their axe and machete, hacked at the heads of the zombies closest to them.

The first one managed to scale the wall and fell clumsily over it. Shawn killed it instantly with a bolt.

I called Andy and Chet back. We stood in a line and paused for a second as four more flopped on to the ground just a few metres away from us.

Andy shouted, "Don't shoot!" and darted forward, using his heavy bladed machete to smash their heads apart before they even managed to get up. As he turned to run back to us another zombie fell over the wall and its momentum made it roll towards him. It seized him by the ankle and tripped him up. As if in slow motion, we all ran forward to help him but just as I was about to stab the creature, it bit deeply into his outstretched calf muscle. I drove the knife home and dragged its carcass away. Then Chet and I dragged Andy clear.

He was screaming in pain and anger. Stricken, we all looked at each other. There was nothing we could do; he'd been bitten and to all intents and purposes, he was already dead.

Andy knew this only too well.

More zombies were managing to clamber over the wall now, so we were forced to ignore Andy for the moment. There were now about ten of the things, all rising to their feet and lurching towards us, and more were coming over all the time.

As they clumsily pulled themselves over, they dislodged stones from the top of the wall, making it even easier for the ones that were following.

We were in serious trouble. I wasn't sure we'd be able to re-load quickly enough to get them all in time.

Behind us I heard a hoarse shout. "Look after yourselves, everyone; it's been a hell of an adventure! Chet, you've been a good mate. I love you like a brother. You'll get through this."

I was almost knocked flying as Andy barged past me. Swinging his machete with a yell, he launched himself at the nearest zombie, almost decapitating it with his first blow. His wounded leg forgotten, he pushed, kicked and slashed his way into the middle of them. Their attention was now fully focused on Andy and they all began to converge on him.

"Fuckers!" yelled Chet, tears streaming down his cheeks.

Stepping forward, he swung his axe into the back of the nearest zombie's head while its attention was focused on his friend.

We couldn't see Andy now, but we could hear him swearing and shouting, as the zombies formed a tight circle around him. Then his shouting turned to roars of pain, and the last glimpse I caught was of him swinging his machete into the head of one of them while another tore into his neck.

The sudden silence, apart from the sound of the zombies snarling and clothing tearing, made us realise that it was all over. But he'd given us a fighting chance. The zombies had eyes only for the place where he had fallen. Rage and a thirst for vengeance seemed to take over, and screaming and swearing, Shawn and I hurled ourselves into the battle with Chet.

I looked round at a sudden scream from Becky and realised that the three of us were in danger of being surrounded. Without stopping to think, I launched myself at the nearest one and kicked at it viciously until it fell over.

Then I grabbed Chet and Shawn by their shirts and dragged them through the gap I'd created. The shotgun was still lying where I'd dropped it. I snatched it up and assessed the damage.

Over half of them were dead. The last few were still stupidly struggling over the wall, which was now in poor shape as half of it had crumbled. A group of them was still feeding greedily on Andy's corpse but the rest had now turned their attention back to us.

It must all have happened in a space of about ten minutes, but I was absolutely exhausted. Sweat was pouring down my face and my arms felt like lead. Wearily, I re-loaded and shot two more. We weren't going to make it. Louise fired her weapon and Shawn and I looked at each other. He looked just like I felt. He just gave a shrug and fired his crossbow at another target.

Without looking back, I shouted, "Becky, get the kids into the car. Remember, I love you. Don't try to help, just get them somewhere safe."

The sound of my children screaming in anguish ripped at my heart, but I couldn't look back. I had to buy them enough time to get away.

"Kids, be brave for Mommy," I called, tears pouring down my face. I prepared to take out as many as I could.

Now we were nine, but for how much longer?

Chapter twenty two

Our backs touched my car. I heard Becky start it and registered the sound of the kids crying inside. Louise, Chet, Shawn and I formed a semi-circle. I shot my last two cartridges. There wasn't enough room to swing the gun effectively, so I threw it down and pulled my knife back out of its sheath, holding it ready.

"I'm really sorry, guys, I thought we'd get through this," was all I could say before the words stuck in my throat. I heard a crack and watched stupidly as the head of the zombie closest to Louise exploded. I recovered enough to kill the one nearest to me with my knife, then watched in astonishment as the one next to it collapsed with a hole in the front of its head and the brains sprayed out of a gaping hole in the back of it.

I didn't dare look behind me. There were too many zombies closing in on us. We were still fighting for our lives, but I could see more dropping in my peripheral vision. Someone out there was helping us, and it couldn't have come at a better time. We'd been seconds away from being overrun and slaughtered.

The wall of dead zombies we'd created kept the others away from us, and the ones attempting to grab us from behind were steadily being thinned out by our unknown saviours, making it much easier for us to kill them.

I looked for another one to kill, but all at once there were none. Every zombie was dead and the ground was littered with their bodies, all lying in heaps at grotesque angles.

The only sound to be heard was our laboured breathing and the engine of my car.

The engine stopped and I heard the window wind down. I turned to see Becky and Maud sitting in the front of the car and the three children looking at me from the rear seats. They sat there silently, still looking petrified.

The quiet sound of a sheep baaing on the moor sounded positively unnatural after what we'd just experienced. Who had just helped us?

"We're coming out from behind the wall. Lower your weapons," came a shout.

I lowered my knife and Shawn and Louise followed suit. Two soldiers in full kit with rifles aimed at us stood up from behind the wall to our left.

One of them kept his weapon trained on us while the other climbed over the wall. The other followed, and they walked slowly towards us. At a command from one of them, they both lowered their weapons.

They stood in silence for a moment, then the older one of the two broke into a smile and said, "That was a bit intense, wasn't it? I'm glad most of you made it."

We were speechless.

Chet finally spoke first. "How long have you been there? Could you have saved my mate?"

The man shook his head. "No, pal. I'm sorry but we couldn't. In fact, if it wasn't for him we wouldn't have got involved. I'd made the decision, rightly or wrongly, not to intervene when we first came across you. Your situation looked so hopeless I didn't want to put us at risk for no reason. It was only when we saw what he did - sacrificing himself to help you, even though he'd been bitten - that I decided you must be OK and worth helping.

That man was a fucking hero the way he piled in there. If anything like that happens to me, I hope I go down as well as he did. And then the way you all piled in after him! I just had to help after that."

He grinned and then put out his hand. "Sorry, I'm forgetting myself. I'm Sergeant Simon Wood and this scrawny individual by my side is Marine Brown."

Still stunned by their appearance, I stammered, "Hi ... er sorry, but where the hell have you just come from? I mean, thanks for helping us out and everything. I really thought we'd had it then. But, well, you just rise up from behind a wall and say, 'sorry I wasn't going to get involved, but then I decided I would!' I'm a bit confused!"

He laughed. "Yes it sounds like it. Let me explain where we came from." He looked beyond us towards the car. "Do you want to let the women and children out of the car first?"

Becky, who'd been listening through the car window, leant out and said, "Don't worry, we're getting out, but can you make sure none of those things are still alive first?"

"Good point!" said Shawn.

The soldiers agreed, so we spent the next few minutes kicking each zombie to check for signs of life and if in doubt, throwing in an extra stab to the brain for good measure. Chet made his way over to what was left of Andy. We could only tell it was him by the scraps of clothing that remained.

We let him have a moment to grieve for his friend. I did a quick count-up. He'd gone down fighting and taken six of the bastards with him. Shawn walked round retrieving as many of his crossbow bolts as he could. He was careful to wipe them before packing them away.

We gathered together over by the house, away from the piles of bodies.

Becky ushered Maud and the children into the house. We waited for Chet to join us, then went into the kitchen. The children retired to the lounge and carried on watching the DVD that was still playing. Becky grabbed a carton of juice from the fridge and rummaged through the cupboards for some glasses.

She found a tray, picked up a biscuit tin she'd found on the worktop and carried it all through to the children.

Maud seemed to come to all of a sudden. "Shall I put the kettle on then?"

We looked at each other and everyone burst out laughing. So typically British.

There we were in the middle of a zombie apocalypse, struggling to survive, and fighting off hordes of flesh-eating monsters, one of our fledgling group already eaten alive, and at the first opportunity someone was offering to make a nice cup of tea.

Maud left us all giggling hysterically, and looking slightly mystified, proceeded to make a large pot of tea. Eventually we could laugh no more, but it had served its purpose: we'd managed to release a lot of pent up emotion. I walked over to Maud, wiping the tears from my eyes, and hugged her. "Thank you. We needed that," I told her.

We helped ourselves to steaming mugs of tea and Sergeant Wood told Marine Brown to go outside and keep watch while he told us their story.

They were Royal Marines, based out at Bickleigh Barracks, just outside Plymouth. They'd been out there on a routine training exercise the previous morning when the whole base had suddenly been placed on alert. Amid great confusion, everyone had been issued with live ammunition and squads had been hurriedly formed and dispatched in whatever vehicle was available to guard road junctions.

The only orders they'd received had been to protect citizens against outbreaks of "civil unrest". Their lorry had contained a hastily cobbled together mix of marines from different units under the command of a young lieutenant who'd been told to go to a road junction outside Bodmin.

Shortly afterwards a panic-stricken crowd of people, escaping from Bodmin, had rounded the corner and converged on the soldiers in the hope of being protected. The bemused marines had had no time to react when the snarling mass of zombies surged up against the screaming crowd and tore into them savagely. Not understanding what they were dealing with, some of the soldiers had ventured forward to try to intervene and had been quickly and brutally overrun themselves.

Sergeant Wood, a veteran of many campaigns, had quickly realised that their only chance of survival was to fight back.

He'd ordered the remaining marines to raise their weapons and they'd fired into the growing crowd of undead, who were heading straight for them. By the time the bewildered men had worked out that headshots were the only way to kill them, the zombies were almost on top of them. As they retreated they could only watch helplessly as one by one their comrades were attacked and ripped apart. When there were just the two of them left, Wood and Brown had just managed to scramble into the lorry.

Hastily filling their Bergens with as much ammunition as they could carry, they'd jumped down from the lorry and sprinted away from their pursuers. Being marines, they were both superbly fit and had had no trouble losing them.

Once they were clear of them they'd instinctively headed for the moors, an area they knew well, which they knew they could disappear into. They'd been working their way across the moors, in the hope of returning to their barracks and regrouping with whoever was left, when they'd come across the farmhouse and witnessed the drama that was unfolding.

He apologised again for not immediately coming to our aid, but we waved it off. He had saved our lives and that was all that mattered.

"Do you think anyone will still be alive at your barracks?" asked Becky.

"Well ma'am. If there isn't, then the whole country is fucked as far as I'm concerned. Because if those undead bastards have managed to get through the best trained and toughest soldiers in the world, then there really is no hope. And I guess my carefully planned career will be over and I'll have to look at my early retirement options! But my main objective is just to get back to see if any of my mates got through."

He showed emotion for the first time. "They're the only family I've got."

He stared at the wall for a few moments, then snapping himself out of it, asked how we'd come to be fighting off an army of zombies in the middle of Bodmin Moor. I told him our story and how we'd all come together over the past two days, and that Louise had only joined our group a few hours before. I concluded by describing the plan we'd been formulating to try to head to Warwick Castle as, in our view, it was the only place we could think of where we might stand a chance of surviving this.

He was intrigued. "A castle! I like it! But what are you going to do now?"

"Well," I said, hesitantly, "we can't stay here, that's for certain. We've just discovered that it's nowhere near as safe as we thought. I suppose we should scavenge what we can from here and keep going. I wish we had a few more weapons though. Your rifles really proved their worth just now.

The shotguns are great, but they have to be reasonably close to be effective, and that creates its own problems. There's a .22 rifle in there but I'm not sure how effective that will be."

Simon asked to see the rifle and ammunition. He admired it, remarking that it was a perfectly good weapon and with the load the bullets had, it should be possible to kill with a headshot at a range of 100 metres. In reality, he admitted, that would be a damn fine shot under the circumstances given that you'd be firing it while under attack by zombies. If you could zero the sight on it to fifty to sixty metres, it would be a lethal weapon. He explained that the advantage of the .22 was that the bullets were light. This meant that you could carry a lot of them with you, unlike the 5.56mm bullets his own weapon used which were heavy and therefore limited you as to how much you could take with you.

Unnoticed, Maud had been quietly searching through the cupboards and had quickly made a huge pile of sandwiches. They were just what we needed.

"I don't think I'll ever be any good at fighting those things," she said shuddering, "but the one thing I *can* do is make sure that no one goes hungry."

I was desperately trying to think of a way to persuade Simon and Ben (Marine Brown) to stay with us and join our group. Being Royal Marines, I knew they were among the best trained and toughest soldiers in the world. We badly needed people like that on our side.

But before I could think of the best way to put it to them, Simon asked to be excused for a minute, saying that he wanted to have a word with Ben, who was still outside keeping watch.

His question, when he came back in, could not have made me any happier.

"I've just had a quick chat with Marine Brown and he's in agreement with me. If we're going to survive this, there's going to have to be more than just the two of us. Even though we're still heading back to the barracks, which we hope will still be operating, we're going to have to face up to the possibility that it might have been overrun. If you want you can come with us. I think we could all help each other out. We've seen the way you fight and if the shit hits the fan big style, you'll be great. All we've done is take pot shots from a distance. You badasses have taken it to them with bayonets, just like the 'Walking Dead'!"

Shawn laughed. "Where do you think we learned how to do it?"

Now we were eleven.

Chapter twenty three

While the children stayed inside watching the TV, and Maud kept an eye on them, we all moved outside to continue our discussion.

"Simon, Ben," I began, "you're absolutely right. We need to stay together. The only way we're going to survive this is by strength in numbers. You two are the only ones with military training, but even that won't help you if you get cornered by a pack of them. We need to put together some kind of plan for getting to your base. The cars we have won't be any good if we have to fight through a lot of them, and what happens if we meet more survivors on the way? We only have a few more spaces available."

Shawn spoke up, "Has anyone seen the film 'Tremors'?" He turned and pointed to a large rusty silage trailer sitting outside one of the barns.

We all looked at him blankly.

He raised his eyebrows. "You know! The film where they used a big trailer and a bulldozer to escape from a large man-eating worm. I reckon we could use that trailer there, pull it with the tractor and then we'd have ourselves a pretty invincible zombie-proof ride."

He looked at us all expectantly. "Let's 'A-Team' the tractor and anti-zombie it. I reckon with its hydraulic front arm, we'll easily be able to clear any blockages we find and the trailer will act as a mobile castle. It'll carry the whole lot of us and more, if necessary, plus a lot of supplies." He finished with a big grin on his face.

We all turned and stared at the tractor and trailer.

It would work. It was an absolutely bonkers, crazy idea. BUT it would work. We could meander slowly through the countryside in a mobile castle.

No! It wasn't bonkers or crazy. It was absolutely brilliant.

I slapped Shawn on the back, and Ben and Simon started whistling the theme from the A-Team. It was catchy, and for a brief moment all the men whistled it together until Becky brought us back to reality by saying,

"You bunch of absolute idiots. Why are men such bloody simpletons? We're in the middle of fighting for our very lives and at the thought of playing a bunch of fictional TV characters, you all start looking wistful and suddenly turn into Hannibal or BA or whoever you wanted to be when you were ten. Grow up the lot of you!"

We all looked sheepish. She continued. "You are now basing my survival and the survival of our children on a movie starring a big worm and a series about a bunch of characters whose only contribution to the world was a big black man who said 'FOOL!'"

We tried to be serious, but when Becky said "FOOL!" there were a few sniggers. She had absolutely nailed the accent.

When she'd calmed down she admitted that it wasn't a bad idea and agreed that we should try it.

Making a conscious effort not to laugh, I said, "Right, guys, let's get started. We have a lot to do before we leave. If we get this done we can be off at first light tomorrow morning."

First of all we decided who was doing what, based on their skill levels.

Simon, Shawn, Ben and I had the most practical experience in terms of mechanics and building, so we volunteered to work on the tractor and trailer.

Becky said that with the help of Maud and the children, she would search for and pack up anything we needed from the house.

Chet and Louise agreed to rebuild the partly collapsed perimeter wall and strengthen it as much as they could. Then they would muck in and help wherever they were needed.

With a sense of urgency (we were all conscious that at any time, an unstoppable wave of zombies might appear on the horizon), we set about our tasks.

The tractor looked fairly new and had a good-sized cab and a bucket loader attached to the front. I climbed up into the cab and was overjoyed to find the keys in the ignition. Either the farmer had been forgetful or he'd just been feeling too ill from the virus to worry about it when he'd got home the night before. Either way, it would save a lot of time hunting for the key. It started first time, emitting a quiet but powerful sounding noise. I pulled it out of the shed and backed it up to the silage trailer. I studied the controls for a minute, and having found the right ones, extended the hydraulic arm and attached the hook on the tractor to the eye on the trailer.

As everyone congratulated me, I didn't have the heart to tell them it was pure luck. I gave them all a casual thumbs-up and pulled the trailer forward away from the wall of the barn so that we could get to work on it.

Shawn and Simon were setting up extension cables and carrying various power tools out of the shed. After a quick check of the materials we had available to us, we came up with a plan.

Using steel roof sheets taken from a large pile stacked next to the barn, we would place a skirt of metal roof sheets, reinforced with timber and steel, around both the tractor and the trailer to stop any zombies we encountered from getting under the wheels.

Shawn was reasonably confident that with his limited welding experience he would be able to fabricate a sturdy wedge that would stick out from the front of the tractor's bucket to act as a zombie plough.

With a combination of trial and error and practical experience, the plan began to come together. We were lucky; we had the right tools, materials and skills, and the will to make it happen. As a result, within a few hours the bulk of the work was done.

Shawn still had some ideas for improving his zombie plough but what we'd created, although it might not win any beauty contests, looked fit for purpose.

Leaving Shawn and Ben to carry on with the work, I asked Simon to give me a quick lesson on using the .22 rifle and we walked back into the house.

Becky and Maud had been busy as well. Using the three children as porters, they'd emptied every cupboard and created neat piles of food, clothing and equipment. They were now systematically sorting them into essential and non-essential items.

I retrieved the rifle and we went to the room where the ammunition had been stored. After hunting around we gathered another two hundred and fifty or so shotgun cartridges and over three hundred rounds for the rifle.

I was pleased with the amount we'd managed to find, but Simon pointed out that we'd probably shot over forty cartridges that morning and he and Ben had burned through about fifty rounds in the short time they'd been involved in the fight. It was a sobering thought and although the little pile in front of us was better than nothing, it clearly fell well short of what we would need.

The rifle was a nice looking weapon with a black synthetic stock, a sling and a telescopic sight mounted on the top. A small magazine stuck out from underneath it. I'd found two more empty magazines in the safe.

I listened carefully as Simon explained that it was a semi-auto with a ten-shot magazine. He showed me how to load a magazine with ammunition and how to insert and eject them. Being used to firearms, it was all reasonably familiar, and after only one demonstration, I was able to perform all the basic tasks needed to operate it.

I loaded all the magazines and put the rest in my pocket, then I placed the remaining ammunition in a bag and carried them outside. After a quick discussion we decided against practice-firing the rifle, as we didn't want to attract any unwanted attention.

I found the cartridge bags Louise and I had been using and filled them with as many as they would take, then made sure they were placed within easy reach.

Looking around, I could see that things were definitely moving in the right direction. The wall had now been rebuilt to a reasonable standard, and more timber and metal sheets had been propped up against it at its weakest points. The gates had also received some attention and were now looking strong enough to withstand a ram raid.

Everyone was rotating on lookout duty depending on how hard they'd been working and whether they needed the rest.

Sparks were still flying from the tractor and trailer as Shawn and Ben worked furiously with the welder and various power tools, improving on the work we'd already done.

Propping the guns up so that they were within easy reach, Simon and I turned our attention to the trailer. The interior was a bare rust-covered steel shell, about seven metres long and with sides about two metres high.

Once we were actually standing inside it we realised that you couldn't see out, so we set about fixing a wooden walkway to each side to act as a viewing platform and firing step.

The sides were only thin steel so it wasn't too difficult to do. Before long we had a basic platform running along each side.

I looked at it thoughtfully. "If we strap a tarpaulin over one end and put a load of mattresses or sofa cushions on the deck it wouldn't be too uncomfortable," I suggested.

"Bloody civvies," said Simon with a grin. "I just want to make it impregnable, but you want to make it cosy as well. Try sitting in an un-air-conditioned armoured vehicle on a hard seat for hours at a time, in the heat of an Afghan summer, just waiting for the next IED to blow your bollocks back home. Trust me, being cosy's not something I'm used to experiencing!"

He slapped me on the back. "Can't wait!"

The arrival of Becky and Maud carrying trays laden with more sandwiches and mugs of tea made us all realise how hungry we were, and more importantly, how late in the afternoon it was getting. We'd all been working flat out for hours.

Still taking turns on lookout duty, we picked a part of the grounds where we couldn't see a dead body and we all sat down on the dry ground to eat.

It was the first time we'd all had the chance to chat properly. Shawn explained that the farm still had power. A room off one of the barns was full of large batteries and the house had quite a technical back-up system.

The batteries were continually topped up by the wind turbine and PV panels provided most of the power the house needed. If more was required then it could be pulled from the mains or if that was down, a diesel generator would kick in. In his opinion, it was a state of the art system and the farmer must either have had money to burn or managed to get a generous grant to install it. It was the kind of system most preppers would kill to own.

He shook his head regretfully, "It's a shame we can't take it with us, but I suppose I should be able to scavenge enough stuff to rig up a similar system wherever we end up."

I asked him what he did and he explained that he was an electrical engineer. He'd been working as a jobbing electrician of late, as it suited him, but in the past he'd worked on big projects both at home and abroad, including some long stints on oil rigs.

Starting with myself, I then went round the group, asking what everybody did and what skills they had. I explained that I'd worked in building and property development, and had paid the bills by renting out houses I'd bought and refurbished myself.

Chet was a medical student who'd wanted to specialise in viral research. He explained that the previous year he'd had a summer internship at a laboratory in Birmingham where they'd been working on curing the common cold. He'd found it fascinating.

Simon snorted at this, saying, "It's probably some lab somewhere that's developed this zombie thing. Don't mess with nature. That's what I say!"

Simon had been in the Marines since leaving school. He was now in his mid-forties and could have retired on a full pension but, having tragically lost his wife to cancer a few years previously, retirement didn't have the same appeal as it used to. He'd stayed on, hoping to pass on his experience to the new recruits coming through; the kind of invaluable experience that could only be gained by participating in most of the scrapes the British Army had got itself into over the past twenty five years.

Marine Ben Brown, on the other hand, had only passed selection six months previously. He was still waiting to go on his first active deployment and had been based at Bickleigh barracks since passing selection. A local lad, he had followed his family's tradition of serving in the Marines and was proud that he was the fourth generation of his family to serve.

The two were complete opposites. Simon was a battle-scarred bear of a man who emanated sheer toughness and therefore commanded instant respect wherever he went. Ben was a thin gangly youth who didn't look as if he'd say boo to a goose. But, I reminded myself, he'd passed selection which must make him a very tough and determined individual, so in his case perhaps looks were deceiving.

Louise lived near Cheltenham. She and her sister owned a holiday letting business and had been in the area, assessing new properties to add to their portfolio. I'd heard of their company and Becky and I had rented a holiday cottage through them the previous year, after reading a newspaper article about how successful this "all-woman" venture had been, going from strength to strength based on good old hard work and customer satisfaction. I was impressed. The sisters had built up a sizeable business from scratch with little more than charm and the power of persuasion.

As she talked, she began to think about her sister again and the tears came very quickly, but she managed to recover and soon re-joined the conversation.

We carried on planning the best course of action to take. We all agreed that it would be best to head for Bickleigh Barracks first, to see if anyone was still alive there.

Even in a slow-moving tractor it should only take two to three hours to get there. And if the base was still operational it would offer us the best protection.

I hesitated, then asked, "Simon, if it turns out that there's no one left there, only zombies, what do you want to do then?"

He sat and thought for a while. Then cleared his throat and spoke. "Well, as I said before. If there's nothing left there, then there's nothing left of the Marines. If that turns out to be the case then I might as well stay with you if that's all right. I like your castle idea; I can see it working. So if that's the case, we'll scavenge what we can from the base and head out."

Ben spoke up. "I'll stay with you as well, but I would like to see if my family made it. They live near the barracks in Plymouth."

"Of course, we will," I assured him. "In fact, if this tractor idea works as well as we think it will, we'll need to try and find all our families and friends. Unless we know what's happened to them, not knowing will just tear us apart eventually. Fuel shouldn't be a problem. There's a diesel tank by the barn so we can take a lot with us, and every car on the road should have fuel we can syphon off."

In the end we decided to take my Volvo and the tractor. The Volvo could be used if speed was needed.

Shawn asked permission and I agreed to him making a few modifications to toughen it up a bit, so that it could stand up better to a bit of zombie bashing if necessary.

All he said was, "Don't get upset if you don't like how I pimp your ride." Then he strode off toward the vehicles. Ben went to help him and the rest of us decided to start loading the trailer. Having looked at the growing piles of food and equipment in the dining room, we decided to make some additional adaptions to the trailer. Using timber and boards, we managed to make a deck between the walkways so that all the supplies could be stored underneath.

An hour later we'd finished. We formed a chain and loaded the underdeck of the trailer with a large quantity of tinned food, camping equipment, clothes and blankets. We took cushions from some of the sofas in the house and placed them on the deck and then we fixed a tarpaulin over a third of the trailer to create a shelter. When we tried it out, we were pleased to find that all the adults could see and reach over the sides and the cushions now provided a comfortable resting place.

"Dad," said Stanley, as he stood on tiptoe looking over the side. "You need to make some spears. You don't need to waste ammunition on killing zombies. You could just bash them on the head from up here."

"You bloodthirsty little tyke!" I said, startled. "Where did you get that idea from?" I enquired.

"Well, you said it would be like a mobile castle and I watched a programme that said the spear was the best way of defending a castle when the enemy was trying to climb the walls."

I nodded smiling. "Well done, son, why don't you take your sister and Eddie and go and find some things we can make into spears."

As he walked off looking pleased, I told Simon how he'd saved my life the day before by killing a zombie with his cricket bat. He was amazed.

"The whole fucking lot of you are crazy! Even your son has more balls than I have. I almost shit myself every time I see one, and now you tell me your nipper bashed a zombie's brains in!" He shook his head, "I'm getting too old for this shit."

Shawn returned and announced that he'd finished adapting my car. Did I want to check it out?

Feeling conflicted, I walked over to it and stopped dead. In the twilight, my reasonably new Volvo now looked like something out of a Mad Max movie.

It was covered in corrugated steel up to halfway up its windows. Holes had been cut into the steel so that both doors could be opened. A wedge similar to the one he'd fixed to the bucket on the tractor now stuck out from both the front and the rear of the car. And a tarpaulin was stretched across the roof.

I was so shocked, all I could say was, 'What's the tarpaulin for?'

He replied cheerfully, "It's your escape hatch! I've chopped a hole in the roof so if you're ever surrounded and unable to move, we can pull up beside you in the tractor and you can just climb out and over to us. Simple!"

I sighed heavily. "I hope you know you've just invalidated my warranty! What the hell am I going to do if something goes wrong with it now? I'll never be able to take it back now you've zombie-proofed it."

His face fell and I took pity on him, slapped him on the back and told him not to worry. He'd done a great job and it would now stand up better to whatever life threw at it.

As darkness was swiftly approaching, we sorted out the guard rotas so that two of us would be keeping watch at any one time. Everyone else decided to sleep on the sofas in the lounge. They all agreed that they'd feel safer with everyone in the same room. Mattresses and duvets were dragged from upstairs bedrooms and soon, apart from the people on guard duty, silence descended as, exhausted, everyone fell into a deep sleep.

The night was peaceful and as soon as the sun started to rise on the eastern horizon, we began to get ready for the day ahead.

Chapter twenty four

While Maud started on breakfast, the rest of us finished preparing the vehicles. The delicious smell of bacon and eggs drifted out from the kitchen, making our mouths water and our stomachs rumble.

Stanley, Eddie and Daisy proudly showed us the items they'd collected for making zombie spears. They'd found some long metal bars which, if we could sharpen the points, would make excellent zombie killers. Shawn set to enthusiastically with the grinding wheel on the work bench in the barn, and before long, we had a respectable pile of sharply pointed spears. We let the kids proudly carry them over to the trailer and put them on the deck.

Simon and Ben had refilled their used magazines and cleaned their weapons the previous night. They'd also given us all a quick demonstration on how to fire and load them, just in case.

After a delicious breakfast we were almost ready to go. We filled up the fuel tanks on the tractor and Volvo, then filled as many containers as we could find with extra diesel. We knew that we should be able to syphon fuel from all the abandoned vehicles we'd probably find everywhere, but it seemed sensible to carry as much as we could with us just in case.

Our final task was to secure the house and fix a sign to the front door, explaining where we were heading.

As we pulled out of the yard, we made sure that the gate was securely closed. If other people came across the farm, then with the gate closed and the farmhouse itself secure, hopefully it would remain free of zombies and would provide them with much needed shelter and sanctuary, as it had done us.

I led the way in the Volvo and Ben joined me to ride shotgun. Shawn had volunteered to drive the tractor, so the trailer carried Becky, Stanley, Daisy and Eddie, along with Chet, Louise, Maud and Simon.

It was a good arrangement. I had the shotgun and Ben had his assault rifle. Shawn was well protected in his fortified tractor and therefore just had his crossbow, and Simon's assault rifle and Louise's shotgun meant that the occupants of the zombie-proof "mobile castle" would also be well defended.

We drove slowly along the track. The moors looked beautiful in the early morning light. I was reminded of the local folklore about not being deceived by the beauty of the moors. Most of the tales centred round the dangers of the unpredictable weather. The weather was the least of our worries. Zombies were our concern.

I slowed down and cautiously pulled on to the "B" road at the bottom of the track. We'd planned the route very carefully and intended to drive off the moors and join the A38, then follow it all the way to Plymouth and the barracks.

For the first mile we saw nothing at all, but then we started to come across abandoned vehicles. There were some grim sights.

Most were surrounded by the discarded fragments of human beings, presumably their previous occupants. The closer we got to the edge of the moors, the more death and destruction we discovered. As we turned on to the A38 I was relieved to find it clear. I sped up to about thirty miles per hour for the next few miles, weaving past the odd abandoned car until we came across a huge pile-up that covered both carriageways.

Cars were piled up against each other as a chilling testament to the drivers' desperation to escape from the horror around them.

Many of the cars still contained their owners, snarling and writhing desperately, but held fast by their seat belts. Others shuffled between the cars, looking for more victims.

Shawn's voice spoke through the walkie-talkie. "Guess it's time to test the tractor. Pull out of the way and let's see what this baby can do."

My heart beating fast, I grabbed the radio and replied, "Go for it, mate. We'll follow and back you up."

Reversing out of the way, Ben hauled back the tarpaulin covering the roof of my car, stood up on the seat, cocked his rifle and got ready. I leant my shotgun in the passenger footwell and made sure the cartridge bag was open so that I could load it and help if necessary.

The noise of our engines had proved irresistible to the nearest zombies and they began to move towards us. We watched as Shawn pulled the tractor forward, and angling the bucket upwards to protect the wedge, used it to push vehicles out of the way. Slowly and skilfully he cleared a way through the tangled mass of metal.

The crazy "Mad Max" modifications he'd made to the tractor were brilliant. Not one zombie could get anywhere near it. And if any of them managed to venture close to the trailer they were swiftly dispatched with a quick thrust from a zombie spear. We followed close behind.

We didn't have a spear, and after Ben had shot the first few that came near us, he realised that the adaptations Shawn had made to my car would keep us safe regardless, so he was able to relax a little. Better to save ammunition than try to shoot every zombie that came close.

He stood on the seat with his gun ready, and ignored the ones who tried desperately but ineffectually to claw at the car.

I used the wedge on the front of the car to great effect and managed to clear most of them out of our path. The zombie plough proved very effective and most were just gently pushed out of the way. Even if they fell over, it was strong enough to push them in front of us until either they rolled clear or, when I could feel the weight building up, I used an abandoned vehicle and scraped the plough against it to clear them off it.

The gruesome, writhing scrapheap left over from dragging zombies along the road wasn't something you'd want to look at for long. Some lost arms or legs, which explained the odd bump the car felt as limbs were ripped off torsos and the car wheels ran over them. But unless the head had been crushed or torn off, the things stubbornly refused to die and continued to move, jerking and snapping their teeth, intent on trying to reach us even though we were now out of their reach forever.

The pile-up seemed to go on forever. It was impossible to count the number of cars involved or how many poor souls had either been eaten or turned. The thought of the terror people must have experienced when they found the road blocked and their own exit cut off by the cars behind them, made my blood run cold.

The fact that many of them had panicked and tried to escape anyhow, was obvious from the crazy angles that some of the cars had ended up in. The thought that that could easily have been us sent a chill through me.

Cars had been driven into ditches or lay completely mangled, having attempted to smash through impossibly small gaps. We came across a clear area, where an articulated lorry had tried to use its weight and power to clear its own path.

It had managed to get a few hundred metres before its bid for freedom had failed.

The driver had clearly made a mistake and somehow the lorry had ended up on its side with the cab hanging in mid-air over a viaduct. Shawn kept up a commentary over the radio, telling us to hang back a bit as he needed to do some shuffling backwards and forwards to clear a tricky area, or warning us if there was a particularly high concentration of zombies ahead.

"There's a coach ahead, and it's surrounded by zombies. I think there may be people inside it."

We couldn't see past the path that Shawn was slowly making through the pile-up.

"Almost there," he announced. "I'll try to pull up next to the coach and scrape the zombies away from one side. If you pull up tight behind me that should keep them away for a while at least."

The coach came into view as Shawn pulled the tractor over and we watched as he used the wedge on the bucket to push the zombies that were banging on the side of the coach out of the way. Blood sprayed as some of them burst like overripe fruit when they were caught between the coach and the wedge.

I stopped my car so that the front of the zombie plough was tight up against the back of the trailer. Leaving the engine running, I grabbed my shotgun and stood up on my seat next to Ben, to get a better look at what was going on. The front of the coach was a tangled mess of metal concertinaed into the back of a lorry. At least a hundred zombies were clawing at the sides of the coach, trying to reach whoever was still inside. Looking ahead I could see that we were almost at the end of the record breaking pile-up. A hundred metres ahead, the dual carriageway was clear of vehicles. The coach had almost made it.

Looking behind, I could see the pathway we had cleared. It stretched a few miles into the distance.

The problem was, as well as creating a clear route for us, it had made it easier for the zombies to follow. Hundreds, if not thousands were slowly staggering towards us. We were the freshest meat in the area and our slow and noisy journey had attracted them like flies. They would continue to pursue us until we lost them, or something else attracted their attention.

Becky, Simon, Louise and Chet were all looking over the metal sides of the trailer. "Can you see anyone inside?" I called. "Keep checking behind us. We don't want to hang around for too long. I'm not sure I want to find out if our vehicles will keep us safe against that lot."

Simon leant over the side of the trailer and banged on a side window of the coach, shouting, "Is anyone in there?"

An answering scream of, "Help us!" confirmed our suspicions.

Simon responded immediately and shouted, "Get away from the window!" Then he grabbed one of the home made spears and began to hammer the window with it. The safety glass was hard to break but finally he managed to do enough damage to make it sag in its frame.

He climbed up on to the side of the trailer and kicked the glass repeatedly until it fell into the coach.

As the glass fell in I could see three youths; two lads and a girl, crouching in the rear seats of the coach.

Becky called to them, "It's ok, come on. We'll help you get out of here." I looked behind us and realised that the swelling mass of zombies was now only about fifty metres away.

"Hurry up! We need to get out of here now!" I shouted.

Shawn still had to clear the last hundred metres or so of road and although we felt pretty much invincible in the fortified car and mobile castle, the sight of so many zombies converging on us was making me very nervous.

Ben began to fire his rifle but it was like trying to stop the tide with a sponge. A waste of time.

Chet and Simon were now helping the three teenagers out of the coach. Even though most of the zombies had been crushed into unrecognisable shapes by the tractor's bucket, arms were still reaching out and trying to clutch them as they leaned tentatively out of the window and stepped over to the trailer.

Ben shouting, "Grenade!" made me turn suddenly, just as he threw it into the middle of the heaving mass of undead.

The resulting boom was deafening and the zombies blew apart as the high explosive wreaked havoc. Arms, legs, torsos and a few heads flew up into the air.

"Man, did you see that!" he whooped excitedly. "They fucking came apart!" He reached into the pocket of his jacket and pulled out a second grenade. "One more and that should hold them back," he yelled as he lobbed the next one perfectly into the middle of the throng.

Once again the damage was extensive, yet nothing seemed to stop them.

They had no concept of fear; their only instinct was to get to us. The carnage caused by the two grenades had slowed their progress a little, but they just continued on, slipping heedlessly through entrails and tripping over body parts. But still they came.

As soon as Shawn starting moving the tractor, I jumped back down into my seat and put the car into drive. Then I began to follow him again. In my mirror for as far as I could see, the horizon was filled with hundreds of zombies.

I hoped fervently that Shawn would have no problems clearing the road. As I followed the trailer steadily through the path that it had cleared, I occasionally stopped and reversed the car into the zombies just behind us.

The wedge that Shawn had fixed to the rear of the car did its job and kept knocking them down, at the same time creating enough of an obstacle to slow the pack down and keep them at bay.

Eventually Shawn pushed the last car out of the way and the road ahead was clear. I grabbed the walkie-talkie thankfully. "Well done, mate. Let's keep going for a few miles, then when you think it's safe, we'll stop for a breather."

"Ok," was all I got, as the tractor sped up and we left the scene of devastation behind us and continued down to the A38, towards Plymouth and the barracks.

Now we were fourteen.

Chapter twenty five

The road ahead was reasonably clear and for a few miles we only encountered the odd abandoned car or lorry. Finally we reached the brow of a hill on the dual carriageway, where you could see for a few miles in all directions. Shawn indicated and we pulled over to the side of the road.

Shawn and Simon spent a few minutes scanning the surrounding area with their binoculars, before announcing that the area was clear. As Shawn climbed down from the tractor and Ben and I stepped out of the Volvo, we grabbed the ladder that Chet and Simon were lowering from the trailer, and held it steady so that everyone could climb down.

I gave Becky and the kids a quick hug. The three newcomers hung back from us. Seeing this, Becky beckoned them over.

"Hi," I said. "I'm Tom, Becky's husband. You've met the other ones in the trailer. This is Shawn, the crazy tractor driver and Ben, my wingman, in the Volvo. How long were you in that bus?"

It turned out that they'd spent two nights in there. The three were in their late teens or early twenties and looked tired and grubby. The two lads wore their hair quite long and had the air of public school boys.

They were both wearing what looked like waiters' uniforms and the girl was wearing a chef's uniform complete with white clogs.

"All three of us have summer jobs at the Royal Fowey Yacht Club," one of the boys explained. "Two days ago everything went crazy and people started attacking and biting each other when we were serving breakfast.

We locked ourselves in the kitchen with a coach driver who'd come in through the back door to escape from the ones that were loose in the town. We hid out for most of the day, not knowing what to do.

Everyone in the club was either dead and eaten or they'd turned into a monster. We knew the town was full of them, so we were too scared to leave. Eventually they found out somehow that we were in the kitchen and started to break through the door. We only just managed to escape in time and then we had to run through the town dodging them. We barely made it to Fred's coach!"

Fred, he went on to explain, had turned out to be a very brave man and had driven them through crowds of them, bashing cars out of the way. "We were going really well until Fred shouted that the brakes had failed. Next thing we knew, we'd piled into the back of a lorry and Fred was killed. The emergency exits jammed so we couldn't get out but it wasn't long before those things had us surrounded so we couldn't have got out even if we'd wanted to.

I don't know what we'd have done if you hadn't come along. We can't thank you enough."

The other two heartily agreed and they introduced themselves. The lads were called Noah and Daniel and the girl was called Aggi. They explained that they'd got their jobs due to their parents being members of the yacht club, and apart from wages, they got free room and board at the club and unlimited sailing when they had time. They seemed like pleasant enough kids and had obviously been well brought up.

Naturally they were very thirsty and hungry after two days on the bus with nothing to eat or drink, and they eagerly took everything we had to offer.

As they ate and drank we filled them in on what we knew had happened. They all came from London and were extremely anxious about their families, but we weren't able to offer them much reassurance, given that we thought the zombie outbreak had started there. We told them what our plans were and said that if they wanted to join us, they were welcome.

If the barracks proved to be safe we would stay there. If not, our plan was to head to Warwick Castle and avoid London. We knew that the capital would be a very dangerous place to be.

They accepted what we'd told them, but were just grateful to be safe for the moment and weren't really up to thinking beyond the next few hours.

We were all astonished at how well the vehicles had done. They were all looking a little more battered and dented and of course, they were smeared with blood, but they were clearly still sturdy enough to last a while longer.

Maud brought out a few thermos flasks of coffee she'd made back at the farmhouse and busied herself serving up steaming cups of coffee.

She tried to offer us sandwiches, but having been battered by gruesome sights for the last hour or so, none of us felt up to eating yet, apart from the children who, thankfully, had been unable to see over the sides of the trailer as we pushed, crushed and speared our way through the cars and zombies along the way.

Shawn spread the map out and we double-checked the route we had planned. We weren't even halfway there yet, but hopefully now that we were on the main road and had got through the huge pile-up, the rest of the journey would be less eventful.

"Marine Brown," said Simon strolling up to him, "who the hell authorised the use of hand grenades?"

Ben snapped to attention immediately, "Improvisation and the need to live, Sir!" He paused for a moment, his lips twitching, then added, "I've still got some left, do you want some?"

"Absofuckinglutely, Marine. They worked brilliantly. But let's just use them as a last resort, eh, Marine? We don't know when we'll be resupplied."

Ben reached into his rucksack and laid four grenades on the ground, passing two to Simon and putting the other two in the pockets of his body armour. He then spent the next few minutes refilling his used rifle magazines and pushing them into the right pouches so that they could easily be reached.

The brief rest had worked and we were all ready to get going again. Noah, Daniel and Aggi were going to ride in the trailer, so we held the ladder while they all climbed up. I gave my family another reassuring hug before they also got back in. As Ben and I returned to the Volvo, we could hear Simon and Chet giving the newcomers instructions on how to use one of the zombie spears. That reminded me that we also needed one, so I pulled up alongside the trailer and Ben asked Simon to pass one down.

Leading the way, I kept to a steady thirty miles an hour. Shawn had said that anything over that might cause the trailer to bounce around too much, which would not be pleasant for its occupants.

We were lucky and the road was as clear as we could have hoped. Whenever we came across a zombie, staggering along the road, I slowed down and either used the plough to kill them, or Ben perfected the art of "zombie sticking", managing consistent headshots with his spear at about ten miles an hour.

Where possible, we were following Shawn's ethos of killing every zombie we could, if it was safe to do so. We knew the country was full of millions of them, but we reasoned that every zombie we put down would be one less to worry about.

I had to stop myself when I found myself making a game of hitting them with the zombie plough, or congratulating Ben when he made a skillful kill with his spear.

I'd been getting carried away with the moment and it wasn't until I saw what could only have been a mother and her daughter, both zombies, stumbling along the road, that it brought me back to my senses. They looked uncannily like Becky and Daisy, and it made my stomach churn.

Ben, who had been enjoying himself as well, noticed my change of mood and on a zombie-free stretch of road, sat down in the seat rather than standing on it.

He was a sensitive and sensible young man and immediately felt ashamed when I explained how bad I'd felt when I'd realised I was beginning to enjoy the game of killing them. We were both much more sombre when we came across the next zombies and killed them.

A lesson in humanity learnt.

Chapter twenty six

As we approached the outskirts of Plymouth, I was relieved to find the road still clear. Like the other towns, smoke was curling ominously upwards from various locations in the city as fires burned out of control.

Terrible thoughts popped unbidden into my mind and I imagined having to face an impossible decision. What if you were trapped in a house or flat with your family, unable or too terrified to leave because the streets outside were teeming with zombies? What if you knew that no matter how hard you tried, you'd be unable to protect your loved ones, and they'd be attacked and killed while you tried in vain to fight your way clear? From the windows you'd be able to see the fire getting closer as it burned its inexorable way towards you.

What would you do? Stay and burn to death, or leave and be eaten alive?

Shaking off the thought, I concentrated on the road ahead as I knew we were getting to the potential choke point of the Tamar Suspension Bridge, which linked England to Cornwall. It stood alongside Isambard Kingdom Brunel's beautiful Royal Albert Bridge, which had spanned the river for over a hundred and fifty years.

I warned Shawn via the walkie-talkie that we were approaching the bridge. Once we were over it, the barracks would only be thirty minutes away, providing the road wasn't completely blocked.

As we drove down the hill towards the bridge, I prayed silently that the road would remain clear. Luck was still on our side.

The only zombie I could see was one of the toll booth attendants who, trapped in his glass fronted booth, smashed his head repeatedly and ferociously against the glass in his desperation to get at us as we passed.

We made our way slowly across the bridge and I glanced at the impressive looking railway bridge. I found its solidity and magnificence a comfort amid all the chaos.

I wondered if a train would ever be seen on it again.

About a mile further on we pulled off the A38 and continued up the A386 towards Bickleigh. The fences and barriers along the dual carriageway must have kept the zombies from wandering on to the carriageway because the only zombies we saw as we drove through Plymouth were either still trapped in their cars or were feeding on the corpses of fellow road users beside abandoned or crashed vehicles.

As Ben warned me that we were approaching the turning for the barracks, a zombie in camouflage uniform stumbled into the road in front of us.

"Stop!" screamed Ben. "Jesus! I fucking know him! It's Gaz, one of my mates."

"Gaz" staggered towards us. His ripped uniform showing an arm that was more muscle and bone than flesh, evidence of how he'd been bitten and turned. He was still wearing his tactical vest and had a pistol in a holster attached to his belt. As he reached the vehicle Ben lost his nerve and started to cry. The sight of someone he was obviously close to having turned into a zombie had hit him hard.

"Do you want me to do it?" I asked him quietly as he sat, unable to tear his gaze away from his former friend, who was snarling, the spittle running down his chin and clawing ineffectually at the glass of the window.

I watched as Ben closed his eyes and took a deep breath. "No, thanks," he said, "I've got this."

He stood up and raised his weapon, then quietly said, "See ya, mate," and shot him through the head.

As the gunshot reverberated across the countryside, Simon called to us from the trailer, "Marine Brown. Relieve Marine Butler of his weapons and ammunition. It's not doing him any good now, is it son?"

Ben, his training and discipline kicking back in, pulled himself together, shouted, "Yes, Sarge!" and climbed through the roof of the Volvo. He quickly stripped his friend of his sidearm and holster, and took all the magazines he had in his tactical vest. As he climbed onto the bonnet of the Volvo and scrambled back through the hole in the roof, Simon spoke gently to him across the gap between the vehicles. "Stay on mission, Marine. We may not like what we're about to see, but we have to stay focused or we'll end up like Marine Butler. If we find any more of our mates, or anybody in uniform in fact, remember that it's not them anymore. They'd have wanted us to put an end to their misery, so don't hesitate; just kill them. None of them deserved to have to walk around like that."

We made our way cautiously towards the barracks. At the main gates the piles of corpses told their own story. The gates were open, but the bodies of soldiers, most torn to pieces, and covered in bite marks and injuries, were surrounded by dead zombies riddled with gunshot wounds. It was clear that the guards had been caught unawares and quickly overwhelmed, and that the ones who'd escaped had opened fire on their attackers in an attempt to save their mates.

One zombie, missing its arms and legs, was feeding greedily on the corpse of a guard, its head buried in the entrails of the unfortunate man as it chomped away.

We followed the trail of dead soldiers and bullet-riddled zombies, many still animate but left immobile by the damage the bullets had inflicted, away from the gates and further into the base and gradually the story of a desperate fight for survival unfolded before us.

In complete silence we drove further into the base. After a few hundred metres we began to see weapons lying abandoned on the ground. Most likely they'd been dropped in panic when the ammunition began to run out. Zombies attracted by the noise of our engines began to move towards us.

Each time a zombie in uniform appeared, Simon and Ben quickly and cleanly dispatched it with a well-aimed shot through the head. The barracks had been their home, and they knew most of them, so each shot was preceded by the unfortunate soldier's name being called out in a final farewell.

Civilian zombies were ignored and we left them to follow our vehicles, as we silently let Simon and Ben perform the last duty they could for their friends and colleagues.

Ben shouted to Simon, "Isn't that Lieutenant Smith's wife over there?" and pointed to a female zombie walking towards us across the grass sports field.

I could see Simon waving at us to come closer, so I pulled the car right up next to the trailer. I put the vehicle in park and stood up on the seat so that we could talk.

Sadly he answered, "Yes that's the Lieutenant's wife. It's no good lad, the whole base has gone. We're well and truly fucked now. This place probably had the best defences in the south-west and they rolled right through here. Nobody was trained to deal with this shit and by the time anyone realised, it was just too late. Raising his weapon, he put a bullet through the female zombie's brain, then he smashed his fist against the side of the trailer and let out a string of swear words.

He noticed Becky staring at him and realised that Stanley, Daisy and Eddie were listening to every word. Instantly, he looked ashamed. "I'm sorry, Becky. Sorry, kids. I've just lost my home and I guess my mates were the closest thing to a family I had left. I'll try and hold it back a bit more."

Becky gave him a quick hug. "Don't worry, Simon. They've learned a lot of choice words in the past few days! We just hope they know not to use them." She turned to the children. "Isn't that right, children? It's one thing to know all these grown-up words, but it's another thing to use them."

They all obediently chorused with cheeky little smiles on their faces, "Yes."

The sudden sound of a shot made us all crouch down and start searching for the source.

"Woody, is that you?" a distant voice shouted out.

Simon stood up and looked in the direction the voice had come from. A few figures could be seen standing on the flat roof of a building about one hundred metres away, waving to get our attention.

The building was surrounded by zombies. "Get over there!" Simon shouted excitedly. "I think that's my old mate Dave on the roof."

As Shawn was still in the cab of the tractor and hadn't heard our conversation, I picked up the walkie-talkie and by pointing and gesticulating, identified the building the people were standing on and told him to get over to it.

Having had plenty of practice, he was now a dab hand at using the zombie plough, and he quickly cleared a way through, pushing, scraping and pulverising the zombies until one side of the building was clear. Following in his wake, I used my vehicle to destroy any of the ones he'd missed.

We now knew what our vehicles could do, so the few zombies that remained and began to collect around our vehicles didn't worry us too much. We knew we were safe enough, and unless we were suddenly surrounded by a huge crowd of them, we were confident that the vehicles had the power to get us out of trouble.

Nevertheless, it still wasn't pleasant having them anywhere near us.

Looking up at the building, we could now see five adults and two children looking down on us.

Simon stood in the back of the trailer with a massive grin on his face. "Fuck me! You're obviously too ugly to eat. Is that why you're still here?"

"Come now, Sergeant Wood," one of the men replied. "I'm the disappointed one. I've been sitting up here for two days now, turning down rescue offer after rescue offer because I heard a battalion of Amazonian beauties was on its way. Imagine my disappointment when you turn up looking like a Mad Max reject. Can you move that pile of shit you're riding in along, please. I'm sure they'll be here soon and you'll only put them off."

As he was talking, Simon picked up the ladder from the trailer and extended it so that it reached to the roof. Then he climbed up.

The two men stood facing each other in silence for a moment, then saying nothing, embraced each other. They were obviously good friends, and had made up their minds that they'd never see each other again.

The fact that they'd both survived the impossible and were now reunited brought a lump to everyone's throats.

Simon leaned over the parapet and told us all to climb up. A few zombies were still hovering around the vehicles, but weren't going to present any problems, so Ben and I grabbed our weapons and scrambled from the roof of the Volvo up into the trailer, then began to help everyone climb the ladder.

Twenty one of us gathered on the roof of the building. The seven who had already been up there looked sun burned and exhausted.

Typically, Becky stepped forward. "When did any of you last have anything to eat or drink?"

Simon's friend replied, "We ran out of water yesterday morning and we've had nothing to eat since all this began."

Without even asking, Chet and Louise turned and climbed down the ladder and quickly returned carrying bottles of water, which were eagerly grabbed and drained.

Maud, once more on a mission, began issuing orders to Chet to bring up the portable cooker and various supplies, while we tended to the newest arrivals to our group. While we kept them topped up with water to rehydrate them, she set about boiling more water to make tea, and pouring tins into a saucepan so that they could have their first meal in three days.

The water had a miraculous effect, and in no time they were all looking much better.

Standing next to his friend, Simon made the formal introductions. "Folks, this is Sergeant Dave Eddy; the oldest and the ugliest, but also the best sergeant the Marines have ever had. We've known each other for most of our careers and we've served together many times. He was my best man at my wedding and helped me carry my wife's coffin a few years ago. He's my best friend and if I had to choose anyone to help us survive the situation we're in now, he'd be at the top of the list."

Looking at him, he seemed to be made out of the same mould as Simon. A slightly older, more scarred model.

If a Hollywood studio were looking for someone to play a traditional "hard as nails" Sergeant Major, holding his unit together against all the odds, then Dave Eddy would be the man they'd pick.

Simon introduced us to the rest of the group.

The other two soldiers were Corporal Steve Popley and Marine Jim Ellis and the women and children were Lucy and her six-year-old daughter Emma, and Victoria and her twelve-year-old son Josh.

Between mouthfuls of the hot soup that Maud was spooning out to the ravenous survivors, Dave told us their story. Unwisely, only a handful of soldiers had been left to guard the base while everyone was being dispatched to other areas of the south-west a few days previously.

Soon after the squads had left, panicked and confusing reports of attacks on soldiers had started to come in over the radio, together with urgent requests for more ammunition. It had been clear that whatever was happening wasn't normal.

After a quick meeting with the base commander, they'd decided to dispatch a rescue and relief mission to try to resupply the men who'd either gone silent, or were now sending through desperate requests for help.

The base commander, Lieutenant Colonel Burgum, had chosen to lead the mission himself. He knew that his men were in real trouble and wanted to do everything he could to help them. He loaded up the last few vehicles left at the base with most of the contents of the armoury and drove out of the gate with twenty men.

There had been no more contact with him since that time.

Sergeant Dave Eddy had found himself in charge of the base. He'd been aware that something terrible was happening, but hadn't been able to piece it all together from the wild reports they'd been receiving over the radio. Reports which had now ceased all together.

Just as he was gathering his remaining men together so that they could plan the best course of action to take, the first zombies had arrived at the base's gate.

The pattern was predictable. The first marines they'd encountered had had no idea what was going on and were soon overwhelmed. They were the ones we'd passed at the gate. In desperation, they'd fired into the mass of zombies and had soon run out of ammunition. In spite of their superb training, they were unable to maintain unit cohesion and had found themselves fighting for their lives individually or in small groups.

Dave had found himself with Corporal Popley and Marine Ellis and two other soldiers retreating through the family housing section of the base. Their ammunition was all but exhausted and they were reduced to holding the zombies back with their bayonets attached to their rifles. Victoria and Lucy had spotted them and run out of the house they were hiding in.

Realising that they wouldn't last much longer, Dave had looked round desperately for somewhere safe. Spotting a ladder, they'd put it up against the side of the nearest building and scrambled up it. The other two soldiers had bravely held back the zombies to give everyone time to get up there. When they'd tried to follow, once everyone else was up, the combined weight of the zombies eagerly pressing against it had knocked the ladder over. The young soldiers had been thrown screaming into the pack, and the zombies had been on them before they'd even had a chance to stand up.

The group had spent the last two days watching helplessly as zombies swarmed over the base and systematically flushed people out from their hiding places. The screams and shouts for help had almost driven them insane as they'd witnessed their friends, colleagues and neighbours being attacked and torn apart, or transforming into zombies themselves.

Realising that they were trapped without food and water, Dave admitted that they'd felt their days were numbered and had quickly begun to lose hope.

When they'd first heard and then seen our outrageously modified vehicles slowly trundling through the base, mangling any zombie that got in the way, they'd all assumed that they were hallucinating. It was only when Dave had recognised Simon's distinctive profile that he'd realised they'd been saved.

Our own story, which only covered the events of a few days, still took a good half an hour to tell. So much had happened, even we had a hard time believing that so little time had passed. We finished our story with our plan to make our way to Warwick Castle and told them that they were welcome to join us.

Victoria and Lucy tearfully admitted that their husbands, who had been dispatched with the other soldiers when the base was first put on alert, were almost certainly dead. They opted to stay with us. The three soldiers also agreed to tag along.

We explained that we'd promised every member of the group that we would try to reach their families and extended the same promise to them. Ben then reminded us that he wanted to go and see if his family had made it. As they lived quite close to the base, we decided to start our mission by attempting to rescue Ben's family.

Now we were twenty one.

Chapter twenty seven

Simon and Dave volunteered to go with Ben to find his family. As Shawn was the expert on the tractor, he agreed to drive. Not wanting to put anyone else from our group at risk, we decided that a party of four would be enough. With the trailer for protection, hopefully they wouldn't need any more than that to defend themselves.

As Simon and Dave had the most experience in planning combat missions, the details were left up to them. The first place they wanted to stop at was the armoury, to see if they could get hold of some more ammunition. If that wasn't possible, Dave said he knew of a few places, such as the guardhouse, that should have a small supply of what they needed.

Before they left we transferred some supplies up from the trailer to the roof just in case they encountered a problem and weren't able to make it back for a while.

We made sure that we'd carried up enough food and drink to last us for a few days. If they were away for longer than that, then it was unlikely they'd be coming back and we would all have to get into the Volvo somehow.

We all shook hands with them and wished them luck before they departed. As soon as they were in the trailer, we lifted the ladder back up to the roof.

The groans of the zombies surrounding the tractor and trailer increased in volume and their movements became more frantic, as they sensed that there might be an opportunity for fresh meat.

Shawn started up the tractor and set the zombie plough to the right height, then systematically tore through the pack that had gathered around the front.

The twitching, writhing mass of body parts left in his wake was a testament to the power of his vehicle, which never faltered as it smashed through them.

They had a walkie-talkie with them and we hoped that from our elevated position we'd be able to stay within range of each other as Ben's family home was only a few miles away. Ten minutes later they reported that they'd gained access to the armoury, which had been left open in all the confusion. Although it had been left almost empty because of the rescue mission they'd still been able to pick up some useful stuff for us. As the noise of the tractor's engine faded into the distance, we sat down to get to know the new members of our group. Maud bustled about handing out mugs of tea.

Corporal Popley was in his mid-twenties and had a shock of curly brown hair. Currently single, he'd been in the Marines since leaving school and had been based at Bickleigh for the last six months. His family lived in Worcester so it would be relatively easy to check on them en route to the Castle.

Marine Ellis was just nineteen and had been in the Marines for about a year. He'd been on various postings but hadn't yet seen active service. He was an orphan and therefore had no family to worry about. He was up front about the fact that if he hadn't chosen to join up, he would inevitably have ended up in a life of crime. He'd chosen the Marines after a few scrapes with the police and had successfully turned his life around.

Lucy and Victoria were both thirty. Lucy was a petite brunette and had worked as a classroom assistant in her daughter's primary school and Victoria had worked as a freelance bookkeeper for a few local businesses. She was quite a sturdy woman.

Their children, Emma and Josh, were sitting with Stanley, Daisy and Eddie, who were trying to engage them in conversation.

They were withdrawn and rather quiet, which was completely understandable, given what they'd been through over the past few days. I knew how well our children (I automatically included Eddie now) had coped and how quickly they'd adjusted to all the upheaval and the terrible things they'd seen. I hoped that Emma and Josh would gradually do so as well.

I walked over to the edge of the roof and peered over. This was my first opportunity to be able to study the zombies properly.

We'd encountered hundreds over the past few days, but at those times we'd either been running away from them, running over them or shooting and stabbing them. Let's face it, being scared shitless and thinking you were about to die wasn't very conducive to making a study of them.

I watched them intently. Like flies, the group below was beginning to increase in number, as more of the zombies in the area slowly made their way towards us and gathered at the base of our building.

They seemed instinctively to want to group together. They knew we were up on the roof and could have stood anywhere around the base of the building, but they preferred to coalesce in one location. It was almost as if they understood at some primitive level that collectively, they stood a better chance of catching their prey than if they went after them on their own.

They milled around together, but there was no actual interaction between them. I experimented by throwing an empty tin can off the roof just to the side of the main group.

They reacted instantly to the sound and almost as one large organism, they moved towards it. I continued to watch them. We were going to have to learn a lot more about them if we wanted to survive.

As I wasn't worried about noise, I took the opportunity to zero in my rifle, which I'd taken out of the trailer before the others had left.

I asked Steve and Jim to give me a hand and rested the rifle on the edge of the parapet to keep it steady, then aimed at the head of a zombie that was about fifty metres away and pulled the trigger.

Steve was watching through the scope on his rifle. "Six inches to the right."

Jim took the rifle from me and twisted an adjustment dial on the telescopic sight, then handed it back.

Steve told me to aim for the same one. It staggered slightly as I hit it but carried on walking regardless.

"Twelve inches low." Once again, Jim twisted another dial and handed the rifle back.

This time the zombie crumpled as a small red hole appeared in its forehead.

"Good shot," said Steve grinning, "now try a few more to make sure."

Three carefully aimed shots later, I was confident that I could make consistent headshots from as far out as fifty metres. Conscious that we needed to save our ammunition, I stopped shooting, then reloaded the gun and put it to one side.

Steve and Jim talked about their experiences over the last few days. It turned into a bit of a group therapy session, with all of us describing our most terrifying moments.

The lowest points for them had been having to kill former friends, to avoid being attacked themselves. They'd seen a lot of men hesitate, and pay dearly for it with their lives.

Looking back at my own experiences, I realised how lucky I'd been. I'd faced death a number of times and only survived because Becky, Shawn, and then Stanley had intervened. On the last occasion, if it hadn't been for Simon and Ben, we would all have died. Listening to everyone's stories, it struck me that sooner or later our luck would run out.

We couldn't afford to take any more chances, and if we were to stand any chance of surviving, we needed to get to Warwick Castle as soon as possible. All our hopes and dreams were riding on it being suitable, but it was the best idea we'd been able to come up with. As a theory, it was the glue that was holding us together as a group. It was giving us all a common aim and purpose; something to fight for. So far every new arrival to our group had seemed to grasp this as well.

As I sat there listening to them all, I realised that the plan we had in place was the one thing that was giving everyone some hope that there might be a future. It was something that would make all the horror we would experience on our journey worthwhile.

My train of thought was interrupted by Simon's voice over the walkie-talkie. They were heading back and would be with us in about twenty minutes.

The tone of his voice said much more than that. The news was obviously not good.

We hastily packed up our gear and waited impatiently for them to arrive. Before long we heard the familiar sound of the tractor coming closer.

The zombies below us turned towards the sound and began to shuffle towards it, their primitive thought processes collectively deciding that the approaching noise would provide a better opportunity for finding food than waiting for us to descend.

The tractor didn't slow down. It smashed its way through zombie after zombie until it had cleared a path to us. The plough on the front was looking rather more blood streaked and battered than it had done and Shawn, who up until now, I had thought of as a cautious but skilful driver, seemed to be driving in a fury. The tractor and trailer ground to a halt up against the wall, crushing and dismembering the zombies pinned by its blade. I realised with a shock that I could only see Simon and Dave in the trailer and that Simon, his face twisted in anguish, was holding a small bundle of blankets in his arms.

Shawn switched off the engine and we hastily lowered the ladder so that they could climb up.

Simon appeared first, holding the bundle awkwardly against him, and to our amazement the bundle let out a shrill cry. The bundle was a baby!

Instinctively, the women stepped forward and helped Simon step from the ladder on to the roof.

"Becky, could you hold her for a moment?" he said, as he handed her the crying bundle. The baby was immediately whisked away and all the women started to fuss over it.

As Dave and finally Shawn climbed up the ladder, I handed them the mugs of tea we'd got ready for them.

"What happened?" I asked.

Dave looked at Simon. "You tell him."

Simon took a gulp of his tea and began. "There's not much to say, really. After we'd resupplied with ammo, the journey to Ben's house didn't take long at all. The roads were reasonably clear and we easily dealt with the zombies along the route with our spears." He went quiet for a minute, then continued.

"The housing estate where his family lived was a bit trickier, as there were a lot more of them walking around and on the narrower roads, we had to use the bucket to clear a way through the cars parked on either side. So of course, soon we had quite a crowd following us. When we pulled up outside his house it all looked quiet. The front door was closed and all the curtains were still drawn. We were actually quite hopeful that they'd made it."

He took another gulp of tea, closed his eyes for a second, then carried on.

"We all shouted but got no response, so Shawn sounded the horn on the tractor. Then we heard the baby cry. Ben's got a six-month-old baby sister and we knew it could only be her. Before we could come up with a plan, Ben jumped out of the trailer shouting her name, kicked the door in and went inside."

He paused again and I could see that he was finding it difficult to continue. "Suddenly there were hundreds of the bastards, only thirty metres away, so all we could do was try to hold them back to buy him some time. We shot as many as we could and Shawn started to shunt the tractor backwards and forwards to stop them getting too close, and it worked. We managed to keep them away from the front door. Then Ben came flying out of the house carrying his sister. He threw her up to me and started to climb in himself."

Simon looked up at me now, his eyes moist. "Just as he was about to climb over the edge, he looked back. There was a woman walking out of the house. It was his mom. I met her at a social a few months back so I know it was her. I don't know what Ben was thinking because the woman had clearly turned. Maybe he just saw what he wanted to see. Anyway, he shouted her name and before Dave could grab him, he dropped his weapon and jumped down and went back to her."

We listened appalled, as he finished his story. "I think when he got halfway across the front garden he suddenly came to his senses, because he hesitated and stopped. But by then, because we'd been distracted and stopped firing to help him, and Shawn had stopped moving the tractor so that he could climb up, the zombies had broken through.

They got between us and they trapped him. Dave started firing again but by then there were just too many of them. Ben had his back to his mom and was kicking out at the rest to keep them away so he didn't see her until she grabbed him and bit into his neck. The last thing we heard was him calling for her as she pulled him to the ground."

He sighed. "There was nothing we could do. I threw a grenade at the spot where he'd fallen. I knew he'd rather be blown to kingdom come rather than become one of those things. For fuck's sake, I think we all would."

He looked round at us all, smiling bleakly. "And here we are. One down because of some stupid mistake. He was a fucking good Marine!"

One dead, one new arrival.

We were still twenty-one.

Chapter twenty eight

The baby was called Sarah and was the usual bundle of cuteness that only a six-month-old baby can be. She had a head full of black hair, and judging by the volume of her crying, was in good health. Hungry but healthy.

Louise came over. "She needs food. We've given her water and changed her but she isn't really going to be happy until she's had a bottle."

I looked at everyone. "Any suggestions, guys?"

Straightaway, Vicky said, "There were a few babies on the base. I know where they lived so I could show you. There should be bottles, food and nappies in the houses."

"Great. Let's get going. Who going to come with us, Simon?"

He thought for a moment. "After the shit that happened with Ben, the only way we're going to accomplish anything is by using maximum force to ensure mission success. I say we take every shooter we've got in the hope that we're able to maintain control over any situation we get ourselves into. There's no point in doing anything half cocked; it'll only end up with more of us getting killed until there's none of us left. All or nothing, I say."

Chet said, "Someone needs to stay and protect the ones up here."

Maud put a stop to the discussion. "We don't need protecting up here. They can't reach us. Everyone who needs to go, go and get some food for that poor baby. I'll stay here and look after the children. Just make sure you all come back safe."

Louise and I fetched the shotguns and Shawn was given Ben's rifle. Chet wanted to come too and grabbed the .22 rifle.

The soldiers still had their own assault rifles and sidearms. Noah, Daniel and Aggi also volunteered to come.

Although all we had to offer them was the zombie spears, we figured the more the merrier, and they climbed into the trailer. Vicky agreed to ride in the cab with Shawn so that she could guide him to the houses we needed to get to. As soon as the soldiers had refilled their empty magazines from the ammunition Simon had taken from the armoury, we were ready to go, spurred on by Sarah's plaintive crying. We left one of the walkie-talkies with the group on the roof so that we could still communicate with them.

It was my first time riding in the trailer, and it did make you feel invulnerable looking down at the zombies, swarming around the trailer, before we set off. While Shawn was helping Vicky into the tractor, we gave the three greenest members of our group a quick lesson in using the spears.

To their credit, they didn't hesitate to start killing the ones they could reach by leaning over the side of the trailer. Pretty laudable, as I'm sure that three days before, they would never have dreamed of doing anything so violent.

As we approached the first house, Shawn positioned the trailer so that any zombie that approached the front door could easily be speared as it went by. Simon led the way with the four soldiers, checking and clearing the house of its family of zombie occupants. They'd been trapped in the lounge. It wasn't clear who had turned first, but all that remained of the little girl was her head. After dealing with her parents, who were still feeding on the carcass of her older brother, Simon respectfully placed a blanket over all their remains and shut the door. They'd all known the family.

We used bin liners as carrier bags and hurriedly filled them with as many baby items as we could find. We soon had four bin bags' worth of nappies, sterilising tablets, bottles, baby food and baby clothes. With no other zombies in sight, we took the time to search and strip the house of anything else that might prove useful. We quickly emptied the kitchen cupboards and the pantry of any food. It proved to us that as long as we could avoid zombies, getting supplies wasn't going to be a problem.

Every house in the country would yield a certain amount of food if we were desperate. The supplies we already had would see us through the next few days so we weren't too worried about it yet, but if it was readily available, it seemed sensible to grab what we could. We could carry a lot of supplies in the trailer.

We hadn't yet had a serious discussion about the best place to get any supplies we needed. Food was obviously our primary concern, but most members of the group only possessed the clothes they stood up in, so as daft as it might seem, we'd probably have to fit in a visit to a clothes shop soon as well.

It had been a while since Stanley and Daisy had used baby milk or nappies, so I was a bit out of practice, but I knew the few boxes of milk and packs of nappies we had found should last a six-month-old for quite a few days. We agreed that we had enough for the time being and should get back to the roof so that we could give Sarah the milk she so desperately needed.

On the journey back I was relieved to find that there seemed to be fewer zombies around. We'd killed a lot of them on our initial journey through the base and every time we drove through in the tractor more of them were destroyed, either by being run over or stabbed.

The base was relatively isolated, and we thought it likely that the zombies we'd encountered so far had been from the local village.

Hopefully, the base would remain off the beaten track for zombies for the time being, and receive little attention from any from further afield. I knew this situation wouldn't last, but was grateful for the temporary relief it offered us.

Half an hour later Sarah, full of milk and with a small but hearty belch, fell into a deep sleep. Maud made a cosy bed for her under a tarpaulin shelter which had been quickly and expertly erected by Shawn and Dave. Without even thinking, we all started talking in whispers, casting guilty glances at her if we happened to make too much noise. None of us wanted to be the one who woke her up.

The day was getting on and everyone was exhausted from another day of fighting for our survival. Realising that it was far too late to even contemplate leaving our secure location on the roof, we began to set up camp for the night.

Simon and Dave wanted to return to the armoury so that they could empty it of anything useful. As there were fewer zombies milling around now, they decided to set off straight away. Before that, we formed a chain and passed everything we would need for the night up out of the trailer, in order to make the camp as comfortable as possible. We left a group behind to organise the camp and the rest of us climbed down into the trailer.

All the people who'd been on the previous mission to find baby food had volunteered to come along. The silent bonds of comradeship were already binding us together as a group. We all assumed our previous positions around the edge of the trailer, already feeling like veterans.

After a few minutes of dealing with the zombies who'd begun to converge around the trailer, clawing at its corrugated steel sides with tedious tenacity, there were no more within reach. Shawn started up the tractor and we ploughed through some stragglers that were trying to block his path. The area around our building was beginning to resemble a medieval battlefield. The ground was strewn with broken bodies and body parts. Many had been crushed flat having been driven over on numerous occasions.

The air was thick with flies and although the smell of decay wasn't overpowering yet, it wouldn't take long for the summer sun to change that. That in itself was a good enough reason for us to leave as soon as possible.

The trailer rocked slightly as the large all-terrain tyres rolled over the corpses. As Shawn already knew the way to the armoury, he made straight for it, weaving as he steered the tractor towards as many zombies as he could, to enable us to kill them.

We wanted to prevent them from collecting together in packs. That was when they were at their most dangerous. And of course, Shawn's mantra about killing as many as we could made sense.

The armoury was a small squat building set back from the other buildings on the base. There were few zombies in the immediate area but there were still plenty following us, advancing steadily.

Feeling reasonably secure, we all stepped cautiously down from the trailer. Half of us stayed outside on guard duty, keeping a careful eye on the approaching zombies. Simon and the others made their way inside so that they could retrieve whatever remained. He'd already admitted that there wasn't much left, so it was unlikely to take long.

As we watched the zombies getting closer, Chet mentioned that he'd never fired a .22 rifle before, and asked if he could take a few shots at them to familiarise himself with the weapon.

Shawn added that he wouldn't mind having a go with Ben's rifle, an SA80, so that he too would be familiar with it.

We told Simon what we were going to do, (we didn't want him being alarmed by any sudden shots) and let the group on the roof know using the walkie-talkie. As the zombies continued to move closer, Dave offered to show them both how to use the weapons.

Firing from a standing position proved difficult for them and it took quite a few shots for their first targets to fall. The heavier shot from the SA80 caused considerable damage in the case of bodyshots but the light .22 bullets barely seemed to affect them at all. Only a headshot took them out immediately.

Dave stood beside them and said to no one in particular, "This is the fucking problem, and why we all ran out of ammunition in the first place. It's bloody hard to get a headshot from any distance if you're just in the standing position and not steadying the gun against something. It's even worse if you're running and turning to fire. Then it's down to luck.

We've been trained to shoot centre mass. Those fancy headshots you see in the movies are virtually impossible. In most of the fights I've been in, the amount of ammunition expended per kill is massive, and these fuckers just don't die easily."

He shook his head in frustration. "I hate to say it, but out in the field, unless we have complete superiority of firepower and a lot of ammunition, we're going to be screwed.

In a perfect world and from a nice comfy secure location, any marine should be able to get headshots all day long. But facing a horde of those fucking flesh- eating bastards … well, even the 'ice men' among us are going to be a bit shaky. We need to get some new tactics sorted."

About ten zombies were closing in on us, now only twenty metres away.

I glanced at Shawn, who was becoming increasingly frustrated at how hard it was to kill them. As the range decreased, the kill rate was going up, but it was still taking quite a few shots to kill each one.

Many of them had taken bullets to their arms and legs. Some of them were thrashing frantically about on the ground, while others were still crawling like insects towards us.

"Fuck me," he shouted, exasperated. "It was easier with the crossbow!"

"What do you reckon, Shawn, shall we do this the old-fashioned way?" I said, drawing my knife out of its sheath.

He looked at me and then at the zombies, who were snarling and stretching their arms out in anticipation. In answer, he grinned, slung his new rifle over his back and unsheathed his knife.

"Everyone watch our backs!" I yelled as we stepped forward. While one of us struck out at the nearest zombie, the other one stood close by to protect him. Whenever there were two close together, we both attacked.

I felt strangely confident and for the first time I was thinking clearly. We knew more about them now, and providing there weren't too many of them, they were reasonably easy to kill.

I trusted Shawn to watch my back and I knew he felt the same about me. We worked our way methodically through them, dodging outstretched arms and occasionally kicking one away to give ourselves room to deliver that fatal thrust. I felt as if I was standing outside of myself, watching with calm detachment.

Whenever we'd had to fight zombies before, I'd been utterly terrified. We'd been fighting because we had no other choice, because they'd surrounded us and our only option had been to counter-attack. This time was different. We could have climbed back into the trailer and killed them at a safe distance with the spears. But I knew that what we were doing was an important demonstration to the others of what could be achieved against the zombies. About how we could fight them on our own terms, offensively and not just defensively.

As we fought, those thoughts passed through my mind like lightning. Granted, neither Chet nor Shawn had been familiar enough with their new guns, but still, we'd destroyed more zombies in less time just using our knives.

A knife didn't jam or run out of ammunition.

We finished up by dispatching the ones lying closest to us who were still alive and still trying to reach us despite their horrific gunshot wounds. Dave walked up to us, awe struck.

He slapped us both on the back. "Fuck me! Simon told me for civvies you were hard motherfuckers, but man, that was like watching an episode of 'The Walking Dead'! I'm going to have to get myself a better knife. I just don't think my bayonet's big enough. Let's face it, when the bullets run out that's all we're going to have."

We walked back to the trailer and everyone crowded round, congratulating us. The others were still bringing the last few armfuls of stuff out of the armoury. The pile on the floor didn't look very impressive at all.

"Is that it?" Chet asked, taken aback.

Simon shrugged. "I told you there wasn't much left after the base commander loaded up the lorries and went off to the rescue. We're mainly a training base, not a firing range, so we didn't have much in the way of ammunition or spare weapons to start with."

He thought for a moment. "I suppose I never really thought about it. My job was to make sure that the men in my unit had enough ammunition for whatever task they were carrying out, and that their weapons were in good order.

On active service, you carried as much as you could and if you expended it, there was always more to be had. But back home, apart from the firing ranges, you just had your basic ammo load. The amount available was never an issue, because apart from the ranges, you never had to use any.

There must be warehouses full of it somewhere, but I'm buggered if I know where."

The pile consisted of five metal ammunition cans. Each one was stamped to show that it contained one thousand rounds. There were various other boxes containing different calibre bullets, a small pile of tactical vests and some pistols in holsters. Two shotguns leant up against it all. It wasn't a very impressive haul, but then again, it was more than we'd had ten minutes before.

Dave spoke up, "As I said before, there'll be a few places around the base, and there are plenty of weapons on the ground around here, so we can pick those up. But if the whole country's been affected in the same way, there won't be enough guns or ammunition to make much of a difference. We can't fight them all so we're going to have to get to this castle and see if it's as good as you say it is. As long as we've got enough weapons to clear that place out when we get there what else do we need?"

"You know me, Dave," said Simon, frowning, "I can never have enough ammunition if I'm going out there. Those crazy bastards next to you might prefer using their knives up close and personal, but until I run out of bullets, I plan to keep my distance from those flesh-eating fuckers."

Dave looked at Simon, smiled and whispered loudly, "Pussy!"

Simon laughed, "Absolutely, mate. How else am I going to stay alive? My foolproof plan is to hang back and for once in my life, let you do the work. I've been carrying you for years."

Their good-humoured banter calmed things down. With nothing else to be had from the armoury, we quickly loaded up the trailer with our bounty and headed back to the roof, killing as many zombies as we could on the way.

Chapter twenty nine

On the roof we were greeted by delicious smells from the camping stoves Maud had set up.

Once again, using only the limited supplies we had available, she'd managed to conjure up an excellent meal. She waved off our attempts to thank her, simply saying, "I told you I'll never be any good at fighting them, but I'm damn sure no-one's going hungry in the meantime. And I can look after all the children. I always wanted to be a Grandma. Richard was too selfish to want children …"

It didn't matter who you were. You could always make a difference. Maud's contribution made the group stronger. I'd also seen her in action and if it came to it, I was pretty sure she'd fight like a lioness protecting her cubs.

With twenty one of us on the roof that night, a new problem came to light.

Where could we go to the toilet?

"Number ones" were easy. The men stood at the roof's edge and gleefully used the zombies as target practice. The women had been using a bucket and then pouring it over the edge. But "number twos" were a different matter!

Dave explained that due to the lack of food and water prior to our arrival, going to the toilet hadn't really been an issue. But now everyone had full stomachs and bladders, and we needed to come up with a solution quickly to save people's modesty.

I stamped my foot on the roof. It sounded like it was made from timber and felt. "Shawn, let's get the petrol saw out of the trailer. I've got an idea."

Five minutes later, in a corner of the building, I'd cut a small hole in the roof, exposing the room below.

Using some spare lengths of timber we had and a sheet, Shawn and I knocked up a screen and placed a roll of toilet paper by the entrance. Proudly, we announced that the toilet was now open.

The queue that hastily formed showed that we'd built it just in time.

With everyone now feeling much more comfortable, we sat around in the fading light and planned for the day ahead. At first light, Simon and Dave would take a quick trip around the barracks and try to collect as much ammunition as they could. They'd also gather up as many abandoned weapons as possible, if necessary taking them from the dead.

Shawn kept impressing upon us the need to gather supplies at all times. As he pointed out, you never knew when the next opportunity might arise, so we decided to visit the small general stores on the base and empty them of anything useful.

Fuel was our next pressing concern. We'd refilled the tanks of the tractor and the Volvo from the containers of fuel we'd brought from the farm and we still had some left. Simon and Dave told us that there was a large above ground diesel tank in the vehicle maintenance yard from which we could at least refill our empty containers.

If we found any more containers we could bring more back with us.

The route was easy to plan. We would travel up the A38 until it joined the M5 motorway and then follow it north to our destination. By good fortune, all the places we needed to visit to try to rescue family members were virtually on our route.

Shawn for instance, had lived in Bristol. Even though he had no close family members there, he wanted to see if any of his friends had made it.

He explained that they were all preppers like himself and would make valuable additions to our group.

Louise's family lived on the outskirts of Cheltenham and Steve Popley's family lived outside the centre of Worcester. Using a map we were quickly able to identify their locations.

Although devastated, Noah, Daniel and Aggi quickly acknowledged that it would be impossible to rescue their families, all of whom lived in Central London.

As far as we knew, the outbreak had started there and therefore the streets of the capital would be swarming with millions of zombies. We were nervous enough about the rescue attempts we were going to make in Bristol, Cheltenham and Worcester but these were all places with much smaller populations. As a group, we'd already agreed that if at any stage the majority of the group felt it was too dangerous to continue, we would abort the rescue attempt in question. First and foremost, we needed to look out for ourselves.

All the children had already settled down to sleep, wiped out by another long and stressful day. To their credit, over the course of the day Stanley, Daisy and Eddie had managed to drag both Emma and Josh out of their state of terrified silence, by chatting to them and trying to include them in everything. By the time they'd gone to sleep, they'd even managed a faint smile once or twice.

As the darkness wrapped itself around us, our own conversations subsided as tiredness overtook us all. Becky and I cuddled up next to our kids and we soon drifted off to sleep.

Ten minutes later Sarah woke us all up, crying for her next bottle. Even the zombies at the base of the building seemed to groan in protest at having their rest interrupted, growling and snarling in response.

As the dawn began to show on the eastern horizon, I remembered how tiring young babies can be to look after. Twenty minutes after we were all awake and preparing to leave, Sarah fell into a deep sleep for the first time in five hours.

I looked at the little girl's sleeping face. You couldn't be cross with her. A helpless six-month-old baby girl who'd lost everything. She'd already stolen a small piece of my heart and I think we all looked to her as a kind of mascot: a symbol of hope for the future.

If little Sarah could survive this, then there might be hope for humanity yet. A small hope maybe, but at that moment I think we were willing to take whatever we could get.

As we finished our breakfast of coffee and pancakes, we got ready to start our day. We had no idea how long it was going to take us, but we were beginning the journey we'd first planned on Bodmin Moor. That seemed like a lifetime ago.

We were heading into unknown dangers. Our group had grown to twenty one, including a baby. We'd lost friends and loved ones and watched others die without being able to help them. We'd also killed out of mercy. As far as we knew, we might well be among the last survivors in the UK, but we had survived and we knew how to survive.

Now we were heading for one of the oldest symbols of power in the world. These places had offered shelter and sanctuary to people for centuries.

The designs might have changed and the materials used to build them might have altered, but they'd all been built for one purpose: to keep their occupants safe from the dangers that lurked outside the walls. Over the years countless castles had fallen into disrepair, no longer required for their original purpose. Now times had changed. We needed somewhere that could resist a besieging army of zombies. Nothing built in modern times was going to be able to do that.

We set out on our journey to the only place that could offer us a future.

A symbol of our past.

We were heading to our Zombie Castle.

**THE ZOMBIE CASTLE SERIES WILL CONTINUE
IN ZC TWO**

About the author

Chris Harris was born in South Birmingham in 1971. Apart from a few years in his early twenties he has lived his whole life in the city, and proudly declares himself to be a true "Brummie", born and bred.

He settled in Moseley about fifteen years ago and has become a keen and active member of its thriving community.

He is a loyal and enthusiastic member of Chantry Tennis Club, where he can frequently be seen demonstrating his talents on (and off) the court.

He's also a dedicated supporter of several local music festivals and a number of local charities, and is passionate about supporting the local independent economy (and is therefore a regular at the many local independent pubs and restaurants for which Moseley is rightly famous!).

His early career centred around the building trade, before moving on to property development. Now a family man with a wife and three children, all of whom are very important to him and keep him very busy, he still finds time to pursue his many interests, which include: tennis, skiing, racquet ball, darts, and shooting. He's also been an avid reader throughout his life.

He came late to writing, but feels that it's really ignited something long buried inside him. It's given him an outlet for his imagination and, never one to be short of an opinion or the last word, he's enjoyed the opportunity of "putting this down on paper" in his books.

Follow him on Facebook at Chris Harris Author page

Note from the author

Thank you for reading this far. As I've said in my previous books, if you've enjoyed this one, please leave a review and if you haven't, then please accept my apologies, contact me via my Facebook page and let me know how I could have done it better.

Writing this book was a fantastically enjoyable experience. The fact that it was a zombie book enabled me to dispense with reality and break away from the boundaries and rules that respectable human beings are meant to adhere to.

In the meantime, I would like to say thank you to the following people:

To my family for allowing me the time and space to write. Nicky, Billy and Katie, I love you.

To my volunteer Beta readers who again played an invaluable part in the process. To Paul Berry, Shawn Graveling, Simon Wood (they all love their characters), James Clayton, Edward James and Mark Jones - thank you all very much.

To Sian Abbinnett, my initial proof reader and editor. Our meetings were much more fun than proper work. The memory of the looks we got from people overhearing us trying to describe as many ways to kill a zombie as we could think of with a knife while having a coffee in a local coffee shop still makes me chuckle.

And most of all to you, the person who bought my book and took the time to read it, thank you.

FOLLOW ME ON FACEBOOK
Chris Harris Author page

Printed in Great
Britain
by Amazon